# Being Santa

RICHARD ROBBINS

Quill

Printed in the United States of America

First Printing 2014

ISBN 987-0-9829877-5-9

Quill Publishing
937 Poplar Street
Missoula, MT  59802
(801) 597-6923

## Dedication & Acknowledgments

This book is dedicated to the many people who have read *Becoming Santa* and have asked for a sequel to be written. I thank them for their love and kindness and encouragements, and for allowing me to delve once again into a fantasy that comes alive each time I address it.

I thank my wife Fara for the many times I have interrupted her work or studies to get her advice or input. She never lets me down, and her patience has allowed me to follow what I love to do. I love her with all of my heart.

Ted Stoddard helps me with the editing, and without him I may as well not write. His kindness and service will never be forgotten. I know he is busy, but takes time to help one little beginning author. He is more than an editor—he is a true friend.

My distributor, Brigham Distributing, and its owner Alan Smith, have helped get my books into the hands of the public. Their diligence and dedication to take an active part in the success of each book will always be appreciated.

When a printer becomes much more than just a printer, but a person who shows personal interest in your project, and makes suggestions and changes that enhance your work so much, he must be remembered. Thank you Bryan Crockett of Book Printers of Utah, for the care you take in presenting my work.

# Chapters

1. Being Santa ........................ 1
2. Unfinished Business ................. 7
3. Christmas the Year Around .......... 13
4. Mrs. B ............................. 19
5. Santa's Self-Analysis ............... 23
6. Moments of Inspiration ............. 27
7. Real Elves ......................... 31
8. Givers Tidings ..................... 33
9. Sarah's Love ....................... 39
10. The Making of an Elf .............. 43
11. Mr. Martin Burgess ................ 45
12. Elf Induction ..................... 49
13. Country Lunch with the Carters .... 55
14. Call to Elfdom .................... 61
15. Kate, Our New Mall Elf ............ 67
16. Martin's Good News ................ 71
17. New Cars for Old .................. 75
18. A Prayer for Martin ............... 79
19. Santa's New Sleigh ................ 81
20. Committed Elves ................... 85
21. The Art of Giving Gifts ........... 89
22. The Elf Ceremony .................. 97
23. Kate's Performance ............... 103
24. Recognizing Needs ............... 107

25. *Chris's Bible* · · · · · · · · · · · · · · · · · · · · · 113
26. *Christmas Preparation* · · · · · · · · · · · · · 119
27. *Every Little Helps* · · · · · · · · · · · · · · · · · 123
28. *Empathy* · · · · · · · · · · · · · · · · · · · · · · · · 127
29. *Mable's Project* · · · · · · · · · · · · · · · · · · · 131
30. *New Elf, New Costume* · · · · · · · · · · · · · 137
31. *A New Dad for Christmas* · · · · · · · · · · · 143
32. *Company Party Agenda* · · · · · · · · · · · · · 147
33. *Being Kind to Others* · · · · · · · · · · · · · · 151
34. *The Candy Shop* · · · · · · · · · · · · · · · · · · 155
35. *Our Christmas Baby* · · · · · · · · · · · · · · · 159
36. *My 65th Christmas* · · · · · · · · · · · · · · · · 171
37. *Mrs. B's Reward* · · · · · · · · · · · · · · · · · · · 175
38. *Little Things Mean A Lot* · · · · · · · · · · · · 181
39. *Good Hospital News* · · · · · · · · · · · · · · · · 185
40. *A Thanksgiving Kickoff* · · · · · · · · · · · · · 187
41. *Our First Day at the Mall* · · · · · · · · · · · 191
42. *A Santa Solution* · · · · · · · · · · · · · · · · · · 199
43. *The Token of Appreciation* · · · · · · · · · · · 203
44. *Childhood Repentance* · · · · · · · · · · · · · · 205
45. *A Company Party* · · · · · · · · · · · · · · · · · · 209
46. *Haley's Surprise* · · · · · · · · · · · · · · · · · · · 211
47. *Leap of Faith* · · · · · · · · · · · · · · · · · · · · · 215
48. *Annual Christmas Hospital Visit* · · · · · · 217
49. *A Special Last Mall Day* · · · · · · · · · · · · 223
50. *Christmas Eve Day* · · · · · · · · · · · · · · · · 231
51. *Being Santa* · · · · · · · · · · · · · · · · · · · · · · 245

# 1

## Being Santa

It was the morning of January 6th, the day I had set to start my brand-new year as the real Santa Claus. I turned over in bed and, as usual, Sarah was already up and around. I could hear her puttering in the kitchen. I threw on a robe and went to find her.

I could never figure out how she always looked so beautiful and well-kept in the morning. My hair just went all over the place, and I felt a little bad that I didn't always look my best for her.

I just wanted to start this day off right, which included a hug from my wife. She was always free with her hugs, and I never tired of how they made me feel. I can honestly say I never got a hug that I felt was insincere. She loved to hug.

As I put my arms around her she looked up and said, "I love you," and I said, "I love you more." My day had now started out right.

All I had to do from now on was get up every day for the rest of my life and be Santa Claus, which was a 24–7 job. I had so enjoyed my brief introduction to this life that I looked forward to what each day would have in store for me. I knew that the better Santa I was, the more I would enjoy this work. I don't know if anyone can even call it work. I had no specific job description to perform daily, and I had no one to whom I had to answer. The job literally had no labor or toil associated with it, and I felt like all I had to do was follow the promptings of each moment.

I sort of had a picture in my mind of the kind of Santa I should be, and I knew I had a ways to go to get there. I also knew that I hadn't yet even thought about many significant facts about Santa. I realized that two months' experience does not a Santa make. But somehow I didn't feel pressured to make it happen all in one day. After all, in my mind Santa never seemed to let daily stresses enter into his life. I just never pictured Santa as a person who let life reach the difficult stage.

Although I had taken the job of being a Santa to help provide a living for my wife and me, I loved the fact that the job had become much more than that. It had become, in fact, a *raison d'être,* a reason for living, a justification for my existence. It helped make me feel significant—as though I might have a major positive effect on others or discover additional important aspects of life. I felt I actually had something to offer that would allow me to enhance the lives of those I would meet. I hadn't taken long to learn that every time I made a difference in someone else's life, the outcome made a difference in mine. It followed that if I influenced others for good, my life would be significantly improved.

I have always been very cautious about my decisions in life. You can only imagine what goes through a man's mind when he considers a decision as "fanciful" as being Santa Claus. I kept asking myself, *Are you just caught up in the excitement of the adventure, or have you let your emotions rule your judgment?* I'm certain that if I approached true friends or even strangers and declared my determination to be a full-time Santa, they might not have stated it, but they would probably be thinking something like, *Have you lost your mind?*

But nothing I was doing seemed eccentric or even unusual to me. All I had to do was recall each episode I had experienced to date while becoming Santa and everything made sense. Everything I had become seemed good and was consistent with or based on reason. I wasn't too concerned that I may be wrong and that everything I was doing was mainly the outcome of emotions. I have always thought that a person's life should be a balance of emotions and intellect, although the very essence of life seems to be a war between these two elements. I've never believed emotions and intellect have to present a conflict.

Intellect is mental and necessary. In fact, I don't think we can become emotional without a degree of intellectual input. Emotion is usually what gives action to our thoughts and moves us with an excitement or even a passion before anything can be accomplished. I have just thought that people should have enough intelligence to control their emotions.

Though I do think that emotion, more than intellect, endears us to others. I can assure you that the first time I saw Sarah, emotions kicked in long before intellect let me know she was the right girl for me.

As a Santa, my emotions always seemed to reign, and I never did have enough time to gather all the facts I might need about people to really get to know them well. If I waited long enough to gather information on each person to make an intelligent decision, I would usually be too late to effectively act on it.

Once you have made up your mind to love everyone, you first love the person and then determine the why. When I thought, *Do I have enough information about this person to determine how to help him or her, and is he or she deserving or just taking advantage of me?* I always came back to an earlier conclusion: "It's always better to err in favor of generosity." Each individual affected me on a different level, and as I saw a person or heard her or his story, my reactions seemed to always be spontaneous, and most often I felt good later about my spur-of-the-moment decisions.

The reality of these thoughts caused me to focus on an idea that to me was almost startling: *I had actually become Santa!* This wasn't fictional—*I was now Santa!* The thought persisted, and others conceded that I was a person who fit the persona of Santa Claus.

I had proved thus far that people liked me as a Santa, and I loved being Santa. I didn't feel that becoming Santa had been too hard, but continuing to be Santa would be the bigger challenge.

We've always been told to just be ourselves, but this is sometimes difficult when we don't even know who we are in the first place. To be someone else, you have to find who that someone else is. To be Santa, I would have to know Santa, and to know

Santa, I would have to understand him completely. We first have to be real to ourselves before we can be real to others. How many adjustments would have to be made in my personal life before I could be a genuine Santa?

I promised myself that I would do the necessary research and make an honest analysis to know every attribute that Santa has. And once I learned all of his qualities, I would decide how I could implement them in my life. I might have conceded in my heart and mind that this was too difficult. After all, how could one person hope to achieve such a high objective? I would have to reach actual existence; anything less than reality would not be acceptable. Could it even be achieved?

I had learned through my short experience, however, that I had moments when I actually felt and acted like the real Santa Claus. And even those seconds or minutes led me to feel that I could stretch these instances into hours and days—or months or years—or even for ages. After all, my belief is and has always been that any person is just one choice away from being suitable to himself or herself and beneficial to others; they just need to know what the choices are.

My life had changed and I was certain that it was for the better. I was spending a lot more time pondering life, and the more I pondered, the more my thoughts shifted from my life to the lives of others. I felt as though I had started looking at each person as if she or he were one of my own, and I was pleased to find in my own nature that people don't have to be perfect to be loved.

For example, I was simply walking in the aisle of a grocery store on one occasion when I saw coming toward me a fellow who normally would have caused me discomfort. He was dressed poorly and looked weathered and messy—and he was even a little mean looking. I said "Hi," and a big smile came to his face as he said "Hi" back. His demeanor had changed, and his belied appearance was replaced with a certain character that I liked.

I was playing around with some words later that evening while considering this experience, and this little poem came out that expresses the way I was starting to feel:

*I'm just a simple kind of guy.*
*I really don't know the reasons why;*
*I just do things I feel I should,*
*And good comes back like I knew it would.*

*You know, I love the folks I see,*
*And I feel their love come back to me;*
*It doesn't matter who they are*
*Or if they're just a little bizarre.*

*I just smile and then say "Hi," you see,*
*And they smile back and say "Hi" to me;*
*You might have money and all it buys,*
*But I have a lot of smiles and "Hi's."*

*Sometimes they even talk to me*
*And say, "You're as pleasant as can be;"*
*I say, "It's all because of you!"*
*That's all I say; it seems to do.*

*Then they just smile, and so do I,*
*And that's got to be one of my reasons why;*
*I don't know how it would make you feel,*
*But somehow it makes my life more real.*

*So I just smile and then say "Hi," you see.*
*And people smile back and say "Hi" to me;*
*You may have money and all it buys,*
*But I have a lot more smiles and "Hi's."*

*Some look tired, and some look sad,*
*And some look down and some look bad;*
*I just think all some folks need*
*Is someone to give them a little heed!*

*When I say "Hi," some say "Hello."*
*Do they feel better? I'm thinking so;*
*But I think what counts and believe is true—*
*When you say "Hi," you're a better you.*

*So I just smile and say "Hi," you see.*
*Then they smile back and say "Hi" to me;*
*You may have money and all it buys,*
*But I love all my smiles and "Hi's."*

*Their whole face changes when they smile,*
*And they look great for a little while;*
*I hope they say "Hi" to those they see*
*And do to those what they did for me.*

*It makes me feel good when they reply,*
*And I think I know the reason why;*
*This I know, and it feels good to find*
*That just for a second I was on their mind.*

*That's why I smile and say "Hi" you see,*
*Because they smile back and say "Hi" to me;*
*I don't need money and all it buys,*
*But I sure do need my smiles and "Hi's."*

As Santa, I was experiencing a lot of unique feelings, and I was liking myself more for having them. Those outcomes must be part of being Santa. I was becoming more understanding, which gave me a confidence I had never before experienced. I was becoming more reliable. I believe sympathy played a part in this because my interest in people peaked, and I accepted them for who they were. That behavior on my part definitely made me feel kinder toward all.

All of this gave me feelings of elation, which is why I believe Santa is so merry. I found that the joy Santa displays is far short of the joy he feels. You can only imagine such feelings of satisfaction. Santa's spirited nature boosted my energy levels to the point of even being courageous, but at the same time I felt a calm and a peacefulness that comforted me.

The contentment that most people in life seek was ever present, and it gave constant reassurance that I was properly applying myself. I knew that to accomplish all I had to do, I needed to learn to be more considerate, affectionate, sensitive and devoted.

# 2

## Unfinished Business

While I was in this state of thought, Sarah entered the room, gave it the quick once over to see if it needed her attention, looked at me, and in that one look sensed I had been somewhat meditative. She said, "A penny for your thoughts."

I assured her that she wouldn't be getting her money's worth. She gave a little giggle, shrugged her shoulders, picked up a full wastebasket, and walked out of the room. The interruption was welcome and brought me back to reality. I could sit and think all day. Doing so helped me to arrange my ideas, but even perfectly laid-out ideas were just that—plans made, not plans accomplished.

Often, action will solve problems that the intellect can't seem to wrap around. Action has a way of invigorating the mind. I know that our lives are lived mostly in our heads and that we must come to terms with the life in our minds to allow our bodies to function properly. Not until a thought is put into action can the validity of the thought be confirmed.

I recalled what someone once said, that "You cannot plough a field by turning it over in your mind." Upon thinking this, I decided to get back to work. I guess I was thinking so much because I still hadn't determined what I should be doing with myself on a daily basis.

Wanting to start with a clean slate, I decided I should finish up any leftover business from the last Christmas season. I grabbed a pad and pencil. This habit always seemed to give me the green light to think logically. I started making another Santa list:

### Things left undone from the last Christmas:

- *Contact the family that provided the beagle puppy for Tommy.*
- *Check with Dr. Richards to see if Suzy's mother got her teeth fixed.*
- *Figure out what to do for the company that never has a Christmas party.*
- *Write a letter to those whose contributions helped make a meaningful Christmas for so many others. (I decided to make a brief accounting of each person aided and keep the list updated periodically.)*
- *Write letters to the TV station and newspaper to let them know how important their involvement in Christmas had been.*

I first picked up the phone and made a call to the folks who had donated a little beagle puppy to a boy named Tommy for Christmas. The phone was answered on the first ring by the lady of the house. I said, "This is Santa Claus. I was just wondering if everything went all right getting the puppy to Tommy for Christmas."

As though she had been excitedly waiting for my call, she said, "Oh let me tell you about it. It was so wonderful and made our Christmas so meaningful and so much fun. Thanks for letting us help, Santa."

This lady then told me the whole story. Before they took Buddy over (she was calling the dog "Buddy" now) they went to the store and bought a beautiful red dog collar and had the name "Buddy" engraved on a metal plate that was just for that purpose. They picked up perfect dog food for a puppy not knowing if Tommy had any. The lady had sewn a cover for the dog carrier they provided. It was a lovely felt cloth with Christmas designs on it and they would place it over the cage just before going up to the door. The carrier would also make a fine place for Buddy to sleep the first few nights if a bed were not available.

By this time, the woman's husband, upon hearing our conversation, kept adding details she was leaving out. I heard him say, "Tell Santa about the house." I loved how he referenced the conversation to Santa.

She went on to describe a home with a backyard that abutted a little forested area—a perfect place for a dog to have a little running room. By the side of the house was a fenced dog run, and in the far back corner was a doghouse that she said was more like a dog home. Every effort had been made to allow the once-loved pet a comfortable place to live. It was beautifully painted, and over the entry door scrolled in perfect lettering was the name "Buddy." It would make a wonderful home for its successor. Both the lady and her husband were so grateful that their little dog would have a great new home.

They went to the front door with the excitement you would expect from someone who is about to make a person very happy. A boy about 11 years old answered the door, and they asked if he was Tommy.

He said, "I'd better get my parents." He turned around and walked back into the house. It didn't take long to gather his parents, and the three of them soon appeared at the door. The father then kindly asked if he could help them.

The lady told me, "This is where it got fun. I told the family that we were on an errand from Santa Claus and that he had sent us with a gift for Tommy."

They set the carrier just inside the door, and told Tommy that Santa said to open it now because it couldn't wait until Christmas morning. The mother gave Tommy a nod, and he lifted the cover off the carrier. Staring out of the wire door, Buddy gave a little yelp, and Tommy couldn't get him out fast enough. Tommy just held the puppy and started crying. He wasn't just whimpering; he was sobbing.

His father let us know that Tommy had loved the little beagle he had just lost, and that tears were always very close to his eyes.

Buddy was licking up the tears as fast as they were coming. It didn't take long until four adults and one little boy were all crying together. Buddy reacted by letting out a little whine of his own, which started them all laughing. Cries and laughs are never far apart.

The lady then said, "Santa, we told them that you had received Tommy's letter, and, as busy as you were, your request was something you just had to take care of."

It's funny—here I had had this unique experience with two people I didn't even know. I hadn't even been told their first names as yet, but a boy's need had given us a priority in our lives. Tommy's condition, a true sorrow, created a degree of accountability on all our parts as though someone had given us a reason for being responsible. The dedication or the zeal that this giving couple had exhibited confirmed my belief that people will respond to serve a principle.

The principle may exist because of a moral code based on some fundamental or general truth or law, but I firmly believe that it is bequeathed to every human being. I think there is a standard rule, an un-worded decree, that just gives a person directions to follow—always for the good.

I told the couple that I would like to pay for Buddy, but I was told that they had received more for this puppy than the other five they had sold for cash put together. I said to them, "Who do you think got the greatest gift, Tommy or us?" It seemed that we both took a moment to let the idea sink in.

After getting their names and a promise from them to e-mail me a picture of them together and a profuse thanks, we said our good byes. I had earlier decided that I needed an e-mail address and had set up *Santa@NorthPole.com*. Of course, the minute I received their pictures, I would run to the mall and have an elf plaque made that I would deliver. I wanted to meet these kind people personally because that was the pay I got from my job: "Santa perks," I called it.

With the puppy almost taken care of, I turned my attention to the company that never had a Christmas party. I could never seem to find the time to drop in to just wish those at this company a Merry Christmas, and I felt bad because now Christmas was behind us.

The thought came to me, Who says a Christmas party has to be before Christmas? The planning was fun from there on. I knew the owner's name and wrote him a letter:

Dear Mr. Ogletree,

I feel bad that I wasn't able to attend a Christmas party with your fine company. It seems that I was probably as busy as you and your employees were, and I just never got around to wishing you and them a Merry Christmas. Since you all probably have to have lunch daily anyway, would you allow me to provide it for you and your employees on Friday the 17th of January? I'll have it delivered right at twelve noon. I believe you had 12 employees. Please invite their significant others to attend.

I have enclosed a stamped, self-addressed envelope and ask that you please send me an RSVP and confirm the numbers. Tell the employees to come hungry because we will be having a full Christmas dinner. Oh! And by the way, could you wish them all a late Merry Christmas from Santa?

Thank you,

Santa Claus

P.S. Don't worry about tables and chairs. My elves will take care of all the necessary items.

As soon as I received their answer, I would stop by a caterer and order a special Christmas dinner with all the trimmings to make it just right. I wanted the dinner to say "Here we are together. We've put work behind us for just a short time. All of the labor, toil, exertion, and drudgery are set aside so we can just talk and look at each other and enjoy those with whom we work. We have much more to offer than just the job we do. Why we do the work is more important than how we do it. Together, we can change our employment from a way of making a living to a way to make a life."

I excused myself from the party with the excuse that it was a long way to the North Pole, and that I had a lot of toys to make for next year. I decided that a note that could be read would be appropriate, and reminded myself to write one as soon as everything was confirmed.

I could see that to do justice to this endeavor it would take more time than I had now, and I decided I would find some quiet moments later to tackle this project.

While in a writing mood, I penned a letter to the TV station and the newspaper, thanking them for adding a degree of credence to the award given. I added that while giving the news, they were also encouraging others to go and do likewise. I informed them that they had been added to my "nice list."

3

## Christmas the Year Around

I started on a course of thought that I'm sure others have followed. A simple question was formed, but it is often the simple questions that need answers before a person can move on to
greater things.

What is it about Christmas that promotes such a tendency
to help and give to others? For the sake of the world, I wished
that Christmas could come more often and stay longer. There
are those who still humbug its notion, but Christmas itself is the
most effective protest against their gloom.

Sarah and I many Christmases ago were presented with a
Christmas picture frame. The frame was wonderfully edged
with colorful teddy bears, wreaths, holly, wrapped presents, and
even a Christmas tree. It had a nice saying about the spirit of
Christmas inside the frame, but we changed it to read:

> We hang this frame the year around
> To serve as a reminder
> That if Christmas is always on our minds,
> We'll be a little kinder.

We hung the frame in a prominent place in our home, where it
hangs every day of the year, so it could be seen as a reminder to
us to celebrate Christmas all year long.

People have always sought sources for joy and happiness, and although others have tried to inhibit them, their natural instincts cannot be suppressed. Mankind has a natural inclination to engage in joyful pursuits, and Christmas gives them an excuse to make this a joint endeavor. When women and men are united in the pursuit of happiness, this world can be a wonderful place to live.

It gladdens me that we have a reason to be joyful for a short period each year, but it saddens me that as soon as Christmas is over, the joy, the happiness, and the mere gladness of it all is boxed and put away with the garlands, ribbons, and ornamentations. As store windows lose their glitter and homes look plain without their trimmings, the tedium of life takes over, and a dreariness, almost a lifelessness, sets in.

I've always thought that Christmas should generate a strong enough message to motivate us to retain the joy it inspires throughout the rest of the year. The profound lessons life offers us, especially when they are for our good, should be continuously embraced.

It's like going to church on Sunday. Something tells us we should be there, and we feel good about ourselves for making the effort to attend, and once there, when the sermons and lessons are given, we feel good and vow to be a better person. Monday and the rest of the week come along, and by the next Sunday, we have to almost force ourselves to attend again.

The happiness we feel at Christmas time is not coincidental. It takes a lot of planning, and its execution is not without effort. Once happiness is experienced, we like its feeling and use Christmas as an excuse to revive these sensations year after year.

When you pass a custom on from one generation to another, you are actually handing down patterns of behavior, practices, and beliefs that they, your ancestors, know you value. Happiness and joy become continued lessons from earlier family members. That outcome allows our ancestors to continue to influence our lives, and happiness then becomes a result of tradition.

Traditions that have been passed from our predecessors should continue to be honored. In this way, their values become our values. Each year as new customs or behaviors or joys are experienced, they should be added as our offering to the list of family values. As each generation adds its offerings to those already established, eventually, the perfect celebration will be proffered.

A person is often defined by his or her natural aptitudes. Thus, a person is more likely to be happy if he or she has a predisposition to happiness. And happy people are inclined to have a better life and are more likely to cause those around them to be more satisfied.

My first year as Santa had been such a wonderful experience. My life could have ended with the after-the-fact note reading: "And they lived happily ever after." This would have been perfect, but life doesn't end until the final curtain is drawn. We must move on to the next episode. I guess that living happily ever after should be our continued goal, and if each episode of our lives ends happily, we will be living happily ever after.

Could it be that easy? As we are faced with each of life's experiences, whether sad, difficult, or just boring, if we determine a happy ending for them and do all we can to bring them to a joyful conclusion, will we live a life of bliss? By some mysterious force, I had been given my marching orders for the rest of my life. If I took them seriously, I knew I would live happily ever after. I could never quit on a task until I was content with its completion and until those involved were favorably affected.

I have a lot of reasons for living happily the rest of my life. In fact, while meditating, I have asked myself the question, *What right do I have to be so happy while others suffer?* Other than a wife—whose sole purpose is to make me happy, the real answer always comes up, "I have a job that requires me to be happy." My happiness simply depends on how well I do my work. My happiness is in direct proportion to how happy I can make others. It became quite simple to me: if I want to be happier, which includes all of its derivatives—more content, pleased, joyful, satisfied, fortunate, and even luckier—I would have to be a purveyor of these favors to all I can. The more folks I touch with these "blessings," as my wife Sarah calls them, the more I could like and appreciate, relish, love, and delight in life. And besides, I always found it a lot easier to be happy than it is to be sad.

I determined right then and there that I had to get more knowledgeable on many subjects. The thought came to me, *I have the job; all I have to do now is learn how to do it.* I'd already found out that on-the-job experience is the best teacher, but every time I helped a person, I had asked myself, *Was there something more I could have done?*

Just as I started asking myself where I should begin with my education, Sarah walked in. She said, "You know you skipped breakfast, don't you?" The thought had never entered my mind, and it was almost 1 p.m. She added, "Isn't Santa supposed to have a round belly?" She then set a sandwich on the desk.

It seemed like I was taking a lot of my meals lately in the office. Besides bringing my favorite sandwich—cream cheese, avocados, and bacon—she always made my meals inviting. This time, there was a small bunch of grapes and a few carrot wedges. She thought a meal had to have color to be beneficial.

I gave her a one-armed thank-you hug around the waist as she set down a glass of milk. She paused for a moment and gave me the look that is always followed by a question. As usual, she didn't ask until I prompted her query. When I asked what was on her mind, she stated, "Are you going to keep the beard?"

The mere asking of the question led me to believe there was a reason I should consider it. The first question that came to my mind was, *Why shouldn't I have the beard?* The only answer I could come up with was that I didn't want to draw any unwanted attention to myself. Are there those who would recognize me when I was just out and about? If so, would Santa's character be diminished in any way?

Sarah once again solved the dilemma with one remark: "I suppose if someone needs Santa's help, it wouldn't be proper to make them wait until you could grow your beard in."

I thought to myself, *How much of a part does a beard play in making Santa believable?* I knew from experience that children believed more in a Santa with a real beard than they did in one with what I called a phony beard. Phony beard, phony Santa. My beard had been pulled more than once to confirm my authenticity. So the problem was solved, but so that it would never come up again, I planted the thought into my mind, *I have never seen a shaved Santa, and I don't want to be the one to start that precedent.*

# RICHARD ROBBINS

# 4

## Mrs. B

I had come to a conclusion about the beard, but my contemplation was stopped anyway by the phone's ringing. Sarah used this to excuse herself, and I picked up the phone. I soon found out that planning what to do as Santa was unnecessary. Rather, planning how to do everything that should be done seemed from then on to be Santa's biggest concern.

The call was from a young man. He was hesitant and seemed a little unsure of himself as he asked, "Is this Santa Claus?" He then added that he had gotten my phone number from the newspaper article about the man who had given the wing to the hospital, and then he said something that endeared himself to me. He said, "Do I have to believe in Santa to ask him for help?"

I quenched a laugh, for I could tell he was calling about something he deemed to be very serious. I assured him that Santa's main function was not to make people believe in him. It was for Santa to believe in people, and he liked to help out where he could.

The young man let out a little breath and added, "I knew I was calling the right person." He told me his name was Mark Peterson.

I was expecting a personal problem—something he needed help with. But I was more than impressed as his story unfolded. He was a junior in high school and let me know that all of his

RICHARD ROBBINS

experiences in school had not been what you would call exemplary. Over time he had felt himself drifting and described this as a bad experience. He felt that this descent was unstoppable and had begun to lose friends. Even his family was becoming distanced from him.

He assured me that he now had all of this under control and that it was not for himself he was calling. He then said that he needed my help because of "Mrs. B," who turned out to be Mrs. Burningham, who had taught at his school for most of her life.

He told me that Mrs. B was the first to notice his decline, and in her own way took steps to help him. She would single him out in class and ask him questions that needed thought but that had evident, logical answers. As he pondered these questions that had several right answers and gave his conclusions, she would always lavish praise on him and build his confidence. She made him look good in front of his classmates.

He reminded me that she wasn't easy and demanded superior work but gave superior help to not only him but all the students. She was 65 years old now and near retirement. His fondness for this teacher was very evident. The thing that impressed me was that he recognized where his life would be without her help.

I congratulated him for what he had accomplished and for the fact that he not only changed but also had learned the great principle of appreciation. I couldn't imagine what kind of help this fine young man needed but felt it had something to do with an indebtedness. He then got to the problem: he had learned that Mrs. B had contracted a very serious cancer.

At first, it was more than he could process. He was about to lose the one person whom he felt cared for him more than anyone in the world. It was only after two or three visits to her that he became somewhat consoled. She convinced him that we all will die, and that it is not as important when we die as it is how we'll die. She explained to him that she didn't mean the physical way we will be taken but the mental state we will be in. When she told him she could go with a sense of accomplishment, he knew exactly what she meant. And that made sense to him.

He then got to the real reason for his call. "I have contacted many of Mrs. B's past students and found them to have had the same experience and dilemma that I have," he said. "How do you say thanks to a person like this? No matter what we do, it won't be enough."

I assured him that he was facing the question of the ages: "How do you pay back a person whose greatest gift to you is love?"

After a pause, he came up with what I considered the only right answer. He said, "You could just love them back."

The next questions seemed natural, and the answers seemed effortless. I asked, "How do you love them back?"

He said, "By helping them, being there for them."

Next I asked, "What is the best way to help or serve them?" I expanded on that by telling him there are many ways of serving an ill person but that you can do only so much for them and then they will be gone. Then I asked, "How then will you serve them?"

The right answer was easy for him, and with a degree of understanding and perception beyond his years, he answered, "By serving others."

I replied, "Then it seems that the best gift you can give Mrs. B is plain."

And in a pondering, meditative way, he then said, "We must give her the gift that we will serve others the rest of our lives as she has served us." We seemed to be on the right track.

I next asked him, "How is the best way to do that?"

He answered, "It is simple. We will make a pledge to her. Santa, will you write the pledge for us? The way you wrote and presented the token to Mr. Harrison was very impressive."

I simply answered, "Do you want Mrs. B to have *my* pledge or *yours*?"

His answer was short, "Mine"—and then added, "Ours."

I didn't intend to give him any ideas, and I didn't even tell him how or where this gift should be presented. But I did get a promise that he would send me a copy of the pledge and a time and place it would be presented. I in turn would look it over and make any recommendations I might have. After a profuse thanks for helping him see the obvious, we ended the call.

I stopped what I was doing for a while and pondered what had just happened. I found myself with tears. Wondering why I was crying, I came to the conclusion that there were good people all around. That knowledge had moved me. The fact that I could be of help and seemed to receive help myself from some unknown source with wisdom I could never claim was very gratifying. Mrs. B came to my mind, and I thought to myself, *How much difference can one person make in a community?*

I had to do the math. In its simplest form, the outcome amazed me. Mrs. B taught in high school. With six classes a day with approximately 30 students per class over a 35-year career, it added up to about 6,300 students. They get married and affect 6,300 spouses, and they have an average of three children. That ends up being possibly 31,500 people who have been influenced by Mrs. B.

I went into Sarah and told her the whole story and she told me that I should write all of these happenings down. She added, "Is there a chance we could meet Mrs. B?"

I had thought earlier that I would like to get to know a person like that, and maybe an occasion might present itself for that to happen. Sarah seemed to be caught up into herself for just a minute and then came out with one of her gems. She said, to herself more than anyone else, "It seems that the best gifts are those that can't be paid back."

# 5

## *Santa's Self-Analysis*

After Sarah left, I settled back into the work of the day. In review, I was amazed at what had already happened in just over a half day. My first thought was how much fun I was having—not fun in the way of humoring myself but fun in the way of enjoying and fulfilling myself. That's the best kind of fun.

I had just experienced a very touching event. In fact, in the short time I had been Santa, these events had become almost regular occurrences and always deserved a degree of contemplation. Most of my reflections were introspective. I found myself making a very intense self-analysis. I had changed so much in the matter of a couple of months that I was concerned with what I had done with my life before all of this happened.

*Can just putting on a Santa suit make a person so different?* I certainly cannot remember doing this much good previously in my life. I felt somewhat consoled that I had been a good person, but I had never gone out of my way to be the way I was now. As for being wise and clever and maybe even intelligent, or at least sensible, I had never thought of these as attributes I had displayed throughout my life, and now they seemed like daily occurrences. Maybe I hit on the exact answer to my meditation; maybe it was the Santa suit.

In life, we dress differently for every occasion. Can you imagine being a golfer without the proper attire? When players put on a football uniform, they become almost invincible. When

I function in a church position, a suit and tie let others know I'm serious and even solemn about partaking in my church duties.

I think of Santa when he is not doing Santa duties, and I picture him in his colorful work clothes. I see him going about his busy work schedule making toys, making lists, and feeding the reindeer—but rarely holding a child on his knee or giving presents or advice. When he puts on his suit, he is all business. He doesn't have an office to work in. All he has is a suit that says, "I'm ready and open for business. I'm Santa, and I'm here to make your life more joyful."

When we see a football player all decked out, we expect to see the player perform great feats of athleticism, and we expect a certain performance from him and honor him for his prowess.

We expect no less from Santa. He has to be jovial and cheery and especially optimistic. No problem is too big for him. We never consider the fact that he has had no training. Oh yes, I found out that Santa training schools are located all over the country, but I have never seen a person approach a Santa and ask him for his credentials.

Being Santa became very important to me. I didn't want to just be the Santa person. I wanted to be *Santa*. Being the Santa person is just taking on the personage, looking and acting like Santa; but being Santa is taking on the attributes, and having the loving and caring disposition of Santa. In other words, it is not as important that you are a being, as it is what you are being.

I knew I couldn't just take on all of these attributes overnight, but with the above in mind, I found that over time, all the traits needed would come into place. If I remained alert and even made a study of Santa's qualities and characteristics, I might be able to speed up the process and increase my competence.

I had almost a whole year before another Christmas season began. If I used my time properly, I should be able to increase my effectiveness significantly.

I've always reminded myself that Christmas is the reason for my existence and that Christmas exists for one reason—to celebrate the birth of our Savior. Santa's involvement with this was to enhance the celebration portion of this event. I thought to myself, *There never was a greater reason for celebration.* I have always heard people say, "Let's not forget the real purpose for Christmas." It is almost as though they believe that any frivolity or merriment is out of place. I have always believed that any remembrances of this great occasion are in harmony with the reasons we celebrate. Whether they were parties, galas, festivities, commemorations, or memorials, all were proper.

I could never imagine a Christmas without the solemnity of Handel's *Messiah*, and just as important to me was the story told in the song, "Rudolph the Red Nosed Reindeer." A *Christmas Carol* by Dickens always brought me great joy and resolve to be a better person, but no more so than *How The Grinch Stole Christmas* by Dr. Seuss.

I had a difficult time believing that the babe I knew, who was born in a manger and was now grown in stature to be our Savior, the son of God, would not be honored by such attention. I always thought that sometime during this great celebration, the greatest Christmas story, as recorded in the Bible in the book of Luke, chapter two, should be read. Christmas had to be the greatest of all celebrations. To inhibit it in any way would reduce the happiness the Savior meant to bring into the world.

I had several errands to run, and the day was running out. I had to mail my letter to Mr. Ogletree and his company, and I wanted to print several copies of my investor's journal. But somehow, that just didn't sound right; investors are usually those who commit money for financial gain. "Contributors" sounded better because they usually give for a common cause; however, it made it sound like they were just one of many who gave, and I wanted this to be more individualized. It had to pertain to the singular giver. *That's it,* I thought; *I should call it the "The Giver Journal."*

Yet "Journal" didn't sound right either; it sounded more like sending a newspaper or a newsletter. I wanted it to be more personal, not a reporting of data but a chronological history of events of the heart. I spent some time thinking about the proper word to use, the one that would declare the purpose of the reports I would be sending. The season was full of good things that happen to people, and I thought to myself that such things are called *glad tidings*.

I looked up the word *tidings* and found that it meant what I wanted to say: tidings denoted encouragement, information, instructions, lessons, news, and thanks—and still left room for guidance. I'd call it *The Giver Tidings*. I felt good about the name; after all, it also denoted Christmas—a time of glad tidings for all. I decided to work on it later in the evening and prepare to send it to all those who had given.

I wanted to pick up a small journal that I could carry with me at all times. I had opened a document on the computer called "Santa's Journal" where I could record everything I was doing. I wanted a small book to write those things that impressed me, because at any time I otherwise might forget a name or place or an impression I had at the moment.

In the back of the journal, I would save several pages to make notes. I wanted to list items or concepts that I needed to understand better so I could work on them and become more proficient. I already had some listed that I felt I should study: love, giving, understanding, appreciation, empathy, etc.—subjects they don't teach in college.

While at the post office, I would pick up my mail. I was still getting mail and even some contributions once in a while.

6

## Moments of Inspiration

I decided that each day I would set some time aside to have a moment for inspiration. Over time I found that I had to stimulate myself and arouse my senses to what I was doing. I have found no better way of doing this than just going to where I could sit and watch people. I found that I didn't have to take endless time to do this, and it always added motivation and encouragement. I had found that as I grew older, I spent less time listening to what people had to say—I've heard most of it anyway—but I never tired of watching what they did.

My favorite spot was the mall. They had nice benches to sit on, the temperature was always perfect, and there was never a shortage of folks to watch.

I imagined a story for each person I observed. Some were evident, and some I had to make up, but all were inspiring. I never could watch people without being inspired, and it certainly encouraged me in my pursuit.

Once in a while a person needing a rest would sit next to me on the bench. I never had a difficult time starting up a conversation with such individuals. I soon learned that there is no such thing as a worthless conversation. Opinions, ideas, feelings, or just everyday matters from anyone gave life a clarity that might have never previously been known. I also got to know what people liked and how they wanted to be treated. The process certainly helped me to capture the beauty and the rhythm of the community around me.

On one such watching expedition, a beautiful young girl who was dressed as though she had just come from a party walked around the mall corner with her mother. She was performing an impromptu dance that I thought was as beautiful as I had seen in any theater. She seemed to be uninhibited by what she felt. My first thought was that her heart was speaking what she was feeling. I loved that she danced as though no one was watching, and I thought to myself that maybe we shouldn't always try to hide our feelings but should dance in public once in a while. Jubilation seen is jubilation found.

All of this watching brought me to one great truth: The most important person to watch is yourself!

Just as I was rising to leave, an older gentleman sat next to me on the bench and let out a large sigh. I remarked, "Well, it looks like you made it this far."

He said, "I was just wondering how I'm going to get back."

We both had a little laugh over that. He stated that his knees weren't what they used to be. I asked him how long he had been walking on them, and was told it had been 83 years. I mentioned that they had probably lasted longer than most things he had owned, and was assured by him that I was right. He certainly couldn't complain about how well they were designed.

After pondering for a minute, he then stated that he should probably have them taken care of, but wondered if it would be worth it with the time he had left.

I asked him, "How much time is that?"

He said, "Don't know; but it can't be too long."

I said, "Well can you get done what you want to get done the way they are now?"

He gave a little laugh and said, "I don't think I could get done what I want to even if they were fixed."

I said, "I guess it depends on what you want to do."

He told me that he didn't do what he wanted to do even before his knees started giving him trouble.

I said, "If we were only 20 years younger and knew what we know today!"

He said, "*You* are!"

We didn't land on any particular subject, but went on and on, not wanting to interrupt our common need for a friend with a discussion of anything contrary. There was no vanity or competition in our sentiments—just a calm interchange.

I came to the conclusion that we have to live with the lives we have lived. Going back isn't an option, but there are a lot of options to make while going forward. And I also determined that age has nothing to do with it. A little thought came into my mind that I shared with him: "Well, don't try dying until you've died trying."

I arrived home after running all my errands and could smell dinner cooking. Sarah always insisted on a full evening meal, and I could tell from the smell that it was one of my favorites: meatloaf, baked potatoes, green beans, and a fruit salad. I went into the kitchen where I was greeted with a quick hug and a peck on the cheek.

Sarah said, "I didn't know when you would get home, so dinner is not quite ready. And oh! Mable and Ann stopped over with a plate of dinner rolls for us."

By the time dinner was ready, my mouth was watering and I was hungry. Mable makes whole-wheat honey rolls so good that they would make a meal in themselves, and Sarah's meatloaf was perfect in every aspect. It was never dry and the mixture of seasonings and ingredients only improved the taste of the superior meat. I would always choose her meatloaf over any steak.

I expressed special gratitude in my prayer over the blessing of having this great meal, and thanked Heavenly Father for the kind hands that prepared it. After the prayer and before Sarah could ask, I asked her how her day went.

She said: "Well I took out the turkey carcass from the freezer that was left over from our Christmas dinner, and boiled it most of the day. I got four quart bottles of turkey broth from it." She continued, "I did the laundry, arranged our closets, sewed a button on one of your Sunday shirts, did the ironing, and started making a blanket for one of our neighbors."

She then told me about her conversation with Mable and Ann. "They wanted to make sure you were going to be Santa again this year, and if so, wouldn't you be needing a second suit? They reasoned that as much as you wore the one you have, it might wear out pretty fast. And if you had two, they would not only wear out slower, but you could have one cleaned while you wore the other."

Then Sarah said, "I told them that I had thought this over and decided to make you another one, to which they insisted that they be allowed to help. They both said, 'With more time we'll be able to do a much better job.' Mable even mentioned that she had a dream about how to make the perfect Santa suit. I couldn't fathom in my mind how they could make a suit any better than the one I had, but I learned long ago to never question the ability of those three women.'"

# 7

## *Real Elves*

A thought came to me, and I asked Sarah if Ann and Mable were coming over Thursday night as usual for game night. I was told that she didn't see any reason they wouldn't, as they had been coming for years now. I thought to myself, *They are my elves, and they should be involved in this year-round venture. Why should I be the only one anxiously engaged in this work? After all, Santa has full-time elves.*

To date, they knew nothing of my becoming a full-time Santa. And as far as they knew, I would just start up again about Christmas time. They knew nothing of the financial contributions that had been made, and how those resources have increased my capabilities as a Santa. I decided I would make Thursday night the time to disclose my plans. They should know of the contributions I had received, and what prompted my decision to be a full-time, "real" Santa. After all, Santa has always been, as they say today, very transparent—and so he should especially be with his elves!

Once committed, suggestions and help made by women of this caliber could only be advantageous. Their commitment and dedication had already proved to me that a project would be just what they needed in life. I mentioned this proposal to Sarah and asked, "Do you think they would like to help?" and then added as a second thought, "Do you believe they can help?"

She answered, "Robert, they are my two dearest friends."

Just when I thought she was going to say, *I wouldn't want to do anything the hurt our friendship,* she came up with this gem: "They have been waiting for a long time for something just like this to come along. They have so much to offer and they feel like they're just marking time. They would so like a cause to sink their teeth into."

Said and done! I would plan a presentation to my elves for Thursday night. It couldn't be just off the cuff; it had to be a formal invitation made official in a proper manner. I even thought of creating a special solemn ceremony, like the knighting of a person. I had never thought that this Santa "mission" should be taken anything but seriously!

After helping Sarah clean up the dinner and do the dishes, I went into the office to start writing *The Giver Tidings*. I'd write until news time; I always watched the morning and evening news and subscribed to a morning and evening newspaper. I didn't want to miss a story where Santa might be needed to step in and help out.

# 8

## *Givers Tidings*

I wanted to send a note to those who had contributed in any way to make someone's Christmas better. There were so many, and I thought a follow-up to be in order. I thought it appropriate to make a list detailing the story of every giving Christmas experience, believing that it is as important for the giver to benefit from his or her deed as it is for the receiver. Of course I would leave out the receivers' names, but I didn't want to leave out any details. I hoped that as all of these givers found out the blessings their actions had given to others, they would learn that we don't help others without helping ourselves.

The thought came to me that this group of people had handed me money—money that was never meant to be repaid. In reality, this gift given was a part of the person. They had traded their most precious possession, time, for money, and each dollar they make represents a portion of their life. They are, in effect, saying, "I will work so long, so I can give you this much." They are, in fact, giving a portion of their lives.

We are each given the same number of hours per day, and it has to be used in some way. We can't just keep it, and we can't own it. At the end of twenty-four hours, you have to have used twenty-four hours of time. You have to spend it some way, and once it is spent, you can never get it back. As a wise man once said, "Don't count every hour of the day; make every hour of the day count." You can make more money, but you cannot buy more time.

Or you can give your time to someone else. It won't add a second to their lives, but it might brighten the time they have. We know about how much time we are going to have, and the quality of that time is what is important.

I remember an old proverb that says, "If you want to feel rich, just count the things you have that money can't buy." We shorten a person's life, in effect, by receiving from him or her. We can add to their lives by taking some time to give them thanks. I think Christine Warren said it right when she wrote:

> *Time I have only just a minute.*
> *Only sixty seconds in it.*
> *Forced upon me, can't refuse it.*
> *Didn't seek it, didn't choose it.*
> *But it's up to me to use it.*
> *I must suffer if I lose it.*
> *Give account if I abuse it.*
> *Just a tiny little minute,*
> *But eternity is in it.*

I felt it more important to record the feelings than the actual event. Describing a child's joy, the anticipation in a child's eyes of a dream filled, and always the deep sense of gratitude given by a parent—these were the details they needed to hear. It wasn't difficult to recall all these great experiences, and I got somewhat emotional as I was outlining each occasion. I determined to send a copy of The Giver's Tidings to each person who had donated funds. The stories were arranged in a way that would lead them to believe they had contributed to each person listed.

I thought it important for Santa's Giver Tidings to first let each person or entity know the purpose of the tidings. Second, it was important to tell the story of each receiver, and of how the particular gift helped her or him. Third, and probably the most important reason for the tidings, was to give a gift back to the givers—the gift of fulfillment. And last but not least, a great big "thanks" from the real Santa Claus.

*Santa's Giver Tidings*

Everyone who lives has something to give. You are one of these who have chosen to be a giver. If you have received this Giver Tidings, it is because you have been characterized by Santa Claus as a giver. In its plainest meaning, a giver is a good person—a person who is good to other people. It matters not the size of the gift you have given; a small gift may be considered large for some to give. The gift is not in what is given but in the intention of the giver.

Any gift that can bring one moment of happiness to the giver or the receiver is a great gift. These tidings will tell the stories of those you have given to and of how they were helped by your offering. If one degree of wretchedness in the world decreases your happiness, as it should, then one degree of happiness should decrease your wretchedness or unhappiness.

It is truly felt that the main reason a giver gives should not be because of guilt but because of love. It is also a truth that when we reach the point where they who receive the gift love the giver more than the gift, we will have reached our objective.

I then went on to list each giving incident—dwelling naturally on the spirit of the occasion. As mentioned, I did not give names but also did not hold back on any of the difficulties these people were facing. Their needs, though not too different from those of many others, were brought to our attention. They were real, and they needed real solutions.

I hoped that as all these givers discovered the blessings their actions had given to others, they would learn that you don't help others without helping yourself. In all the Christmas stories I had read of Santa, he was forever trying to teach lessons that would make a person's life happier and often went to great lengths to introduce new values into people's lives; therefore, I felt justified in my efforts to do the same.

These people had done so much good by giving of themselves. I let them know that we still had funds to help many more in need, and that I would periodically send them updates to those we have helped. I tagged the journal entries with a song from our church hymnal:

### Have I Done Any Good in the World Today?

*Have I done any good in the world today?*
*Have I helped anyone in need?*
*Have I cheered up the sad and made someone feel glad?*
*If not, I have failed indeed.*

*Has anyone's burden been lighter today?*
*Because I was willing to share?*
*Have the sick and the weary been helped on their way?*
*When they needed my help was I there?*
*(Chorus)*
*Then wake up and do something more*
*Than dream of your mansion above.*
*Doing good, is a pleasure, a joy beyond measure,*
*A blessing of duty and love.*

*There are chances for work all around just now,*
*Opportunities right in our way.*
*Do not let them pass by, saying, "Sometime I'll try,"*
*But go and do something today.*

*'Tis noble of man to work and to give;*
*Love's labor has merit alone.*
*Only he who does something helps others to live.*
*To God each good work will be known.*

(Text and music: Will L. Thompson, 1847–1909)

The help these good people had shared had certainly set me on my course for the future. The ability to help is enhanced when multiplied.

Well, the local news was over, it was 10 p.m., and my first day of a new year as Santa was completed. I guess I would be asking myself many more times in the future, *Was it a good day?*

I soon found that I could not possibly plan an organized day. Every time I made certain plans, an incident presented itself that changed my priorities. I soon found that priorities of daily life change constantly. Something always needs my attention more than what I am doing at the time. And some priorities I just wouldn't mess with—for example, my wife! I always made sure her needs were met as an individual; she took precedence!

The mere immediacy of death helped me sort out my own priorities when it came to my choices of serving God or people. Of course I knew that if you are serving people right, you are only serving God. Money was never the priority that values were. At the end of every day, all I would have to do is think back on my actions of that day, because actions clarify what your actual priorities are. It is then up to you to determine if your priorities are in line with what is of the most importance to you.

Long ago, I had determined to weigh the value of the priorities of the day by reviewing what I had accomplished. I know that when I chose an action, like watching TV, that action became my priority for the time I sat and watched. Other priorities are replaced with that action. What is important is that we don't let lesser priorities replace greater, more important priorities. My rule was: *Don't do second things first.*

# 9

## Sarah's Love

I woke up earlier the next morning. I don't know why, but my waking-up time seemed to be getting earlier each day. I thought, *At this rate, I won't even have to go to bed before long."*

I helped Sarah with the breakfast. I cooked the bacon and eggs while she got the toast and juice and set the table. I never read the newspaper at breakfast; I prefer our conversations and never want Sarah to think that anything was more important to me than she was. Breakfast was never hurried and was our way of protesting against the busy world we lived in.

Our conversation very rarely centered on anything of much importance, but we always learned a little bit more about each other. The main thing is that we took enough time to bring most conversations to a conclusion. We knew each other well.

I went into the office while Sarah started to clean up the kitchen. She had told me long ago that with just two eating, she didn't have much to clean up. She loved to have the kitchen the way she liked it. Two just get in the way of each other anyway. For some reason, she always thought that what I was doing was much more important than her daily chores. I can assure you that my thoughts were just the opposite. I could never do what she does, and her contributions to life were more than anyone could ask for.

What we call the "small jobs in life" are really the jobs that matter—those that keep order and meaning and certainly love as the primary concern, and that "un-complicate" our lives so that the larger concerns can be more easily addressed. I married Sarah knowing I could live with her, only to find out that I couldn't live without her. I'll always be thankful that my wife has a lot better opinion of me than I deserve. She never wastes time looking for perfect love; she just creates it.

I sat at the desk and determined that the first thing I should do is open the mail I had picked up yesterday. Most of the mail consisted of advertisements, but I noticed an envelope from Dr. Bruce Richards, DDS. I opened the envelope and found a letter and several photos. There was even a picture of an X-ray. I unfolded the letter and read:

*Dear Santa,*

*I thought you might like these pictures of Suzy's mom. They are before-and-after shots of her teeth. As you can see, a lot of work was needed.*

*I called Suzy's mom myself the Monday after Christmas, and told her I was calling to make an appointment to have her teeth fixed. She said that she had received Suzy's present, but apologized for her daughter and said, "Whatever arrangements she made with you, we can't afford them."*

*I assured her that this was a gift from her daughter, arranged by Santa Claus, and that there would be no charge for the service. I guaranteed her that everything was taken care of, and that all we had to do now was to stop her teeth from hurting to make Suzy happy.*

*She came in the very next day, and was very wary. Nothing like this had ever happened to her before. Believe it or not, the Christmas season is my slow time, so I had plenty of time to do extensive work on her. Her name is Lorraine, and the picture with the number "1" on it is her before picture. The copy of the X-ray shows the evident work that had to be done to her mouth.*

*You should know Santa, that I truly felt sorry for Lorraine. She had suffered a lot to make sure her family was taken care of, most often forgetting her own needs.*

*Be assured that we treated her as though she were one of our preferred customers. As you can see from the picture numbered "2," she again has a smile on her face and is quite beautiful. I have to tell you there were many tears exchanged—not from the pain of the drill but from the thanks of the heart.*

*Thank you for letting us help. There is still some follow-up work, and we'll see to it that this doesn't happen again. Please feel free to call on us in the future, as we would love to be of help.*

*Bruce Richards*

*P.S. We may find someone in need in the future, but it surely helps to have Santa involved. Do you mind if we call you on such occasions?*

Oh, that I had the talent to give such gifts. I determined that, from now on, I would be freer with what I do possess, and give such as I have. Giving your life for mankind does not mean you have to die. I wrote Dr. Richards a quick note of thanks and let him know that anytime I could help, I would be there for him. I let him know we had funds to help if needed.

There was another check in the mail for $1,000 from a person in Mr. Harrington's investment group, and this check brought Santa's total to $33,000. The note with the check merely stated, "Thanks for letting me be of a little help."

After checking the mail, I went to my computer to check my e-mails. The pictures of the couple who had given the puppy to Tommy were posted along with their names and address. Their pictures told their whole story. They were a very wholesome-looking couple with smiles from ear to ear. I could tell by looking at them that they were friendly, generous, and warm-hearted by nature. Their names were Bruce and La Dawn Carter—just the kind of people I would like to have as elves.

RICHARD ROBBINS

# 10

## The Making of an Elf

I still had time this morning to consider how I would take Mable and Ann from the status of honorary elves to actual elves. What do you do to make a person the genuine thing—in this case, an authentic elf? Honorary was merely symbolic, most often an unsalaried position. I had in mind to make them professional elves. They would become experts in what they do. I had no doubt that they had all the skills necessary for this work. The very years they had spent in helping others were enough to attest to their qualifications. And I wasn't too worried about having to pay them a salary. They had learned long ago that payment comes in many ways and that the best payments were most often not monetary.

So there were many questions I would have to ask myself. The first question was, *Do I even have the right to make someone a full-time real elf? If so, where does this authority come from?* In fact, did I just take it on myself to be Santa, or was there some kind of way I was selected?

I guess there is no official process for making one a real Santa. It was surely not a calling from a burning bush or from an angel appearing. I'd never heard of a government agency that had the responsibility of appointing a Santa, and I know that elections were never required for the position. I guess the main qualification would be to find someone passionate enough to take on the job. The person just needed to be devoted and enthusiastic enough to be qualified. Some may even say foolish enough, and who would question their legitimacy. This reasoning alone gave me the rationale to accept that I had the authority to proceed with this elf-making process. So what would the process be?

I didn't want to get too businesslike, but I thought a mission statement written out would help them and even Sarah and me to understand more what we wanted to accomplish. I would write one out, and once online I would ask for any changes they might have. I wanted them to feel like their suggestions and ideas would be very welcome and that they had freedom to do many things on their own.

I'd have to come back to this line of thinking later. I wanted to run a few errands before it got too late in the day. I wanted to mail my note to Dr. Richards and also take the pictures of Bruce and La Dawn Carter to the trophy shop to have their honorary elf plaque made. I wanted to get it to them as soon as possible while the magic was still in their minds.

I told Sarah I was leaving, and was asked to pick up some milk on the way home. I dropped Dr. Richards' letter in the drive-through mailbox and headed to the mall.

# 11

## Mr. Martin Burgess

I arrived at the Downtown Mall, parked, and walked in as though I owned the place. I went right to the trophy shop where I was greeted as an honored customer. It was evident that I didn't need the Santa suit to be recognized. On being told that I could pick the plaque up the next day, I left and found myself a few minutes later at the courtyard buying a soda.

I felt a tap on my shoulder, and a somewhat familiar-looking woman asked if I was not the mall Santa we had last year. On assuring her that I was, she told me I might like to know that Mr. Burgess, the mall manager I had worked with, was very ill and was waiting for some kind of transplant at the hospital. She told me that he was quite down and could probably use a Santa to cheer him up. She worked with him in the corporate offices.

I thanked her for the information. I had been wondering why he hadn't contacted me, as he had told me that he wanted to discuss this year's Christmas presentation while everything we did was still fresh on our minds. Thinking there was no time like the present, I called Sarah to let her know I'd be a little late. I let her know what had happened and headed for the hospital.

It was the same hospital where I had helped little Mary, and I knew a few of the people who worked there. I got Martin's room number from the information desk and went to his room on the third floor. It appeared that I had him to myself. I walked into the room, and Martin, recognizing me immediately, gave me a big smile.

I said, "I understand you'll be wanting a special gift for Christmas."

He let out a chuckle and asked if he could get it a little early.

Not knowing what type of transplant he needed as yet, in a little more serious tone I asked him what exactly it was that he needed.

When he told me it was a kidney, I was relieved. I had become somewhat of a kidney expert when Sarah's brother found that he needed a kidney transplant. I had studied the process quite thoroughly because I had considered being his donor.

I took my own quick inventory of Martin. He wasn't too old. He told me his health had always been great. I knew he was quite active, as I had always had a difficult time keeping up with him while walking through the mall. I determined in my mind that he was a good candidate for a transplant. As I told him this, he felt my relief and seemed to feel a little better himself. Needless to say, I volunteered one of my kidneys if it matched, and assured him that with all of the foundations that worked to find transplants of any kind, it wouldn't be difficult finding him a new one.

He said, "What are you, some kind of a kidney expert?"

I said, "No, I am Santa Claus, and Santa has to know where to get all kinds of gifts."

He started laughing and said, "I'm glad I know you on a personal basis!"

I let him know that my brother-in-law was back to work in five weeks after his replacement, and it could even be sooner than that once a proper match had been found.

He had many worries but was freely voicing them, and as we considered solutions for each of them, he started to feel better. No one was better than he at the mall; his job was secure.

I told him I would even stop around and talk to Haley's father, the mall manager, to make sure of that. Kidney donors were plentiful; more people were signing up as live donors, and technology had improved the chance of retention by large percentages in cadaver donors. Recoveries were much faster, and with new operating techniques surgery was much less invasive and healing time was shortened.

Martin got a little serious for a moment and thanked me for taking the time to visit him. He said that there had been a lot of doom and gloom around him, and it was nice to have someone with hope to talk to. Then he said something that brought a group of emotions to my mind, heart, and every other part of my body. He said, "Remember when I was first hiring you and I told you that we were closed as a mall on Sundays? I could tell that you were greatly relieved. Later, thinking this through, I determined that you must be a religious man, and didn't want to work on Sundays, as doing so may be against your religion." He then asked, "Am I somewhat right in this observation?"

I told him I wouldn't have been able to take the job if I had had to work on Sundays, because doing so went against my conscience.

He then said, "While I have been lying here, I have been feeling the need to ask God for some help. I believe in Him, but feel I'd be stretching my relationship with him right now by asking him myself. After all the good things I've seen you do, I feel you're probably on pretty good speaking terms with him."

I wanted to tell him that at this stage in his life, God would probably rather hear from him than from me. It's common knowledge to those who believe in God and worship Him daily, that He is more interested in those who don't believe in Him than in those who do. Those who don't talk to God often feel unworthy to do so and because of that, sometimes never will.

I told him I would be honored to say a prayer in his behalf. After a brief instruction as to the nature of the prayer I would be saying, we both closed our eyes together and speaking in his behalf, I asked the Lord to be aware of his condition, noting that he was a good man. I asked the Lord to bless the medical personnel who would be attending him. I then closed by asking that he might be comforted and know that this would be for his good.

After we both said "amen" he thanked me, and I told him I would come and teach him how to pray himself.

I had never anticipated it but learned fast that Santa needed a spiritual side also. I soon learned that Santa had to be ready to help with every aspect of a person's needs and soon found out that spiritual need was likely the most prevalent need people have.

I said my goodbyes to Martin, assuring him I would be back and would be by his side every step of the way. He called after me as I left, and asked if maybe we could talk about Christmas and the mall next time I came. I waved and gave him a thumbs-up in the affirmative. He was smiling, and I felt better.

# 12

## *Elf Induction*

On many occasions when I was approached by an individual with a personal problem, I would, without the person's knowing, try to find out what commandment she or he was not living. The solution then would be to merely get the person to change and live that commandment. It seemed to me that the commandments were not designed to inhibit a person's activities but to help him or her keep life in order.

I knew that bad things can happen to all people, even if they are trying to do what's right.

For example, I had an employee come to me once when I was a personnel manager at the company where I was working. She was quite upset because, as she said, "A lot of the employees in my same category must be receiving much better salaries than me."

When I asked her how she had come to this conclusion, she merely stated, "Well, look at the cars they drive and the nice clothes they wear. I couldn't afford those things."

Good old covetousness had entered in. It was easy to point out that many had worked for the company longer than she had, and some of them didn't have three children to raise as she had. When I asked if she would like to dress better or have three lovely children, she seemed to grasp the concept. All I had to do was teach her to better understand one of the commandments, and her life fell back into order.

Sarah, with her soft heart, wanted a full report on Martin when I returned home. It was important to her that I rehearse every detail so she could program her role into this problem. Sarah had a way of approaching others' problems. She always assumed that they were immediately her problems, and she was probably the only person on earth who could solve them. Sometimes it took only a bowl of soup, but other times she needed to know if laundry needed to be done or if their house needed cleaning. I had seen her organize a whole week of meals to be taken into a family so the family's time could be directed toward the healing of one of its members.

On one occasion, Sarah drove the children to school every morning so the father could stay with the mother who was ill. She hadn't really known some of these family members prior to their problems, but they knew her well, long after.

As I unfolded Martin's story to her, I am sure that in her mind she was determining how best she could help. I couldn't wait to see what she would do, for doing nothing was not a part of this woman's makeup.

After we had dinner, I retired to the office. I had several unfinished, self-appointed assignments to complete and just about enough time to finish them.

I was still waiting for a confirmation on the after-Christmas party, so I would put my follow-up to them on the back burner. I did have to get the elf induction material ready for Ann and Mable, so I spent my time concentrating on that.

A ceremony certainly had to be involved. A ceremony would make it a formal procedure. Once people accept any position, it is good to give them a starting date and a job description to help them feel empowered to go about their work.

I would first have to work on how to present the fact that I considered myself to be the real Santa Claus. Watching their reaction would let me know whether to go on. If the fact were accepted, I would let them know that Santa needs help, and because in all cases those helping Santa were called elves, could they see themselves becoming real elves?

I emphasize "real" because this would mean that they would actually have physical existence as an elf—not in an imaginary state, or the product of a dream, or an imagination, but a tangible existence. I would have to place great emphasis on this concept, as empowering people would, for the lack of a better word, give them all the clout to act as real elves. Their influence would be enhanced.

To let them know that there isn't a lot of difference between an elf and a normal person, I would give them the following definition of an elf: "Elves are thought of generally as a group of beings with magical powers and supernatural beauty, kind to ordinary people, and capable of helping them."

I wrote a mission statement so we could all be on the same page as to what we wanted to accomplish and to give them an idea of who we are. It was a simple statement but made its point. "Our mission is to secure for every person the opportunity of an equally great Christmas."

The elf induction ceremony would, in fact, be a swearing-in where they would take an elf oath. I figured I may be carrying it a little too far, but thought it necessary to stress the importance of the work we were about to undertake together. I also thought it would make it more fun. Some of the things I thought should be covered in the oath were the following:

- *An elf should always be kind to others.*
- *An elf should be charitable and defend the poor and helpless.*
- *An elf should always share experiences with other elves.*
- *Elves should do all in their power to spread joy to the world at Christmas time.*
- *An elf should promise to have fun at all times, and always wear a smile.*

I would have a difficult time waiting for Thursday night. I couldn't wait to see the responses of Mable and Ann, and I knew it would be a fun night.

After the usual routine on Wednesday morning, I headed out to complete the errands I had listed for myself. I went to the Post Office and was surprised that a letter awaited me from Mr. Ogletree.

Wanting to get his reply as soon as possible, I opened the letter. He started off by saying good things about my wonderful idea. He had talked to several of his officers, and they were all excited. He wished I could be there because he would like me to meet his employees. He stated that they were a wonderful group of people. He let me know that there would be 28 in attendance— that is, if I didn't mind if he invited his son and his wife. In fact, even though they were not working with the company, they were considered family by the employees.

I was very happy and would write a letter back to him later. I thought it proper to give him some suggestions for the party.

I went to the trophy shop and picked up Bruce and La Dawn Carter's elf plaque. I would figure a time during the week to deliver it to them. It was fun seeing the plaque again, and it brought back good memories.

On the way to the hospital to visit Martin again, I made a phone call to the Carters and found out they would be home all day tomorrow. I asked them if I could stop by a little before noon.

She said, "Oh come at noon, and I'll have a good country lunch prepared for you."

When I arrived at Martins' hospital room, there was a very beautiful young woman sitting in my chair at the head of his bed.

I said, "Honey, I think you're sitting in my chair."

She looked up and smiled and said, "Just who are you? I thought I knew all of Dad's friends."

Martin had been sleeping but woke up to the conversation and answered his daughter, "Well, Cathy, this is Santa Claus— and not just any Santa Claus. He is the real McCoy."

I could tell that throughout her life, she had been influenced a lot by her father. She laughed freely, and her goodness was evident in her every action. She said, "Well it's great to finally meet the real Santa."

She had his same quick wit and a willingness to experience even the mystical if it offered happiness. She was just a happy person. I asked, "Do you believe in Santa?"

She said, "I do now. I've never doubted my dad."

I told Martin that he looked better today than yesterday and was told they gave him some medications that the nurse said would even make him more handsome. I asked if he had any extras left over. He told me they had completed all the tests and determined exactly what kind of a match he needed. I told him that I would go down and have them take some blood and see if one of my kidneys would work out.

He said, "I can't ask you to do that."

I said, "I'd certainly ask you if I were in your position."

I left and found out from a nurse in the hall that the lab was on the third floor, suite 300. I went down to the lab and told them what I wanted, and my test began. It probably wouldn't be until tomorrow that they would find out the results.

When I got back to Martin's room, I could tell that he and Cathy had been crying. It concerned me, and I asked if everything was all right.

Cathy said, "Everything is too right; that's why we were crying. Your acts of kindness were so natural and spur-of-the-moment that it affected us very deeply. We became very emotional while discussing it."

I took her by the hand and, sitting in my chair, which she had relinquished, told her I was Santa and one of my children needed a gift that I just happened to have. "If I could give your father the gift of life, wouldn't I be fulfilling the very purpose of Christmas?" I said. "After all, Christ was born for one purpose—to give us the gift of life."

She reached for another Kleenex and said, "Maybe you are the real Santa."

I asked Martin if he needed anything and let him know that the lab said they would have the results tomorrow.

He said, "I hope it matches; part of me would then be Santa."

I reminded myself to check back with him when I found out anything. I ate his leftover Jell-O and left.

# 13

## Country Lunch with the Carters

When I got home, I told Sarah all that had happened during the day, showed her the plaque for the Carters, and asked if she would like to drive up there in the morning with me to deliver it.

She said, "I'd love to, but I thought I'd better make a special refreshment to celebrate Mable and Ann's becoming real elves tomorrow night.

In a matter of fact way, I mentioned that I might give one of my kidneys to Martin if it matched his okay. I expected a little disagreement, at least some concern.

She merely said, "Oh that would be so nice of you. I hope you match; maybe if you don't, I will. Males can take female kidneys, can't they?"

I, matter-of-factly, but with a look of wonderment on my face, answered, "I don't know. I'll check up on it." Dinner was served without any further mention of kidneys.

Later while we were lying in bed together, I had a strong urge that Sarah should go to the Carter's with me tomorrow. The urge was probably prompted by the fact that we weren't going out much together lately. I found out upon asking that Sarah was still somewhat awake, and I told her that the Carters were making a country lunch for me tomorrow, and that I would not only appreciate her companionship but longed for it. "A country drive with a country lunch would probably do us both a lot of good, and it's only 15 miles out of town. We would be back in plenty of time to prepare for Ann and Mable." I committed myself to helping her.

She said, "I think you're right. It's been a while since we went anywhere together."

I told Sarah I would call the Carters in the morning and let them know that Mrs. Santa would be accompanying me. I got almost a little giddy at the idea of spending the day with my wife.

Earlier, I had gone to my office and written a letter to Mr. Ogletree:

Dear Mr. Ogletree,

I was so happy when I received your letter. I'll have my elves—a catering company—contact you with all the information for preparations. If I might make just a few suggestions for making this a successful occasion:

Greetings by yourself, making certain that they know this is a Christmas party.

Once everyone is seated for dinner, have them sing a Christmas carol.

Instead of telling what they want for Christmas, have them tell what they received.

A Christmas quiz with prizes is needed; I'll have the catering company bring a few prizes to award. You could give a prize for anyone who could name all the reindeer, to anyone who could say the second line of "Twas The Night Before Christmas," and the name of the city in "How the Grinch Stole Christmas." We could have someone sing the introduction to "Jingle Bells."

Santa

I didn't know if this would work, but I made the suggestion that he tell them to just take their time and enjoy their meal because they would have the rest of the day off.

I let Mr. Ogletree know that before the party was over, the employees should know each other much better—to the point of being proud of whom they worked with and even for. I added, "Your business is very important to these people; it provides them a way to make a living. The more they know and care for each other, the better they will work together. The reason for work takes on a whole new meaning when the well-being of others is considered."

And then I asked him if he could read the following letter from Santa:

Dear Employees,

It is not wrong to celebrate Christmas after Christmas is over; in fact, Christmas can be celebrated at any time during the year and should be celebrated all year long. Christmas is meant to be the celebration of the birth of our Savior; to limit that to one day would be wrong. The best way to celebrate this occasion is to spread the love that He taught us to those we associate with daily.

Mr. Ogletree speaks very highly of his employees. In his words, he called you a group of very wonderful people. Take some time during this dinner to get to know each other better. Introduce whoever you bring to your colleagues so they can enjoy the stories you bring home about them. A happy workplace is a place where each of you knows each other and sincerely cares and works together where needed.

Have a continued Merry Christmas throughout the year.

Santa Claus

The next morning, I had enough time to finish the plans for the induction of Ann and Mable into the Order of the Elves. Sarah and I wouldn't have to leave until 11 a.m., which would leave me just enough time for a quick hospital visit to Martin. I told him I didn't have any news on the kidney match as yet, but he told me that a nurse had told him they may have found a match anyway. I let him know that I had to drive into the country for a couple of hours, but would check back on him in the morning. His spirit seemed to be very high.

It is amazing how quickly we can get out of the city and into the country. Most of the country was covered with a beautiful January snow that had fallen recently, and we were quite taken by the beauty it spread over the country.

Sarah was one to always point out each little nuance of nature. She said, "Does the snow seem whiter this year?"

Not wanting to spoil the moment, I said, "Honey, I think you're right."

She next saw a squirrel scampering across a snowfield and wondered if its little feet got cold. I said that it didn't seem to be in a hurry and seemed to be having some fun running across such flat ground.

It wasn't long before we saw a sign with an arrow pointing to the Carter's ranch. We followed a rather narrow road for some time. Lined by beautiful fields, the road looked like it had just been plowed that morning. The road wound around a nice little pond that was totally frozen over. In as pretty a setting I had ever seen, on the other side of the pond was a house with a large barn on one side and what looked like a large workshop on the other. I said to Sarah, "It looks like a perfect Santa's workshop."

Before we even reached the house and stopped the car, two people came out of their front door to meet us. I recognized them from their photo. It was Bruce and La Dawn. I could tell just from looking at them that this would be a nice visit.

Sarah said, "Oh, aren't they just lovely?"

La Dawn, whom we soon found out was the spokesman for the family, laughed and said, "I just can't believe that we are actually having Santa Claus and Mrs. Claus at our home for lunch. Everything is ready. Just come in and make yourselves at home."

The aroma from the kitchen let us know we were in for a treat. I could smell fresh rolls and soon found out that ranchers eat lunch a little differently than city folks. I noticed roast beef served with mashed potatoes and gravy and a variety of fresh vegetables, several types of homemade jams and jellies on the table, and even a small dish of horseradish, for no roast beef is complete without it. The milk we drank seemed fresh out of the cow and still had a little foam on it.

We were invited to join them in a blessing on the food and then dug in. The conversation soon turned to Tommy and Buddy.

La Dawn said, "It almost makes you want to just raise give-away puppies."

Bruce very seriously said, "It was one of the best experiences of our lives. Tommy is going to come this summer, and he'll spend a week with us and help us with the ranch. We told him someone had to ride the horses and help mow the hay."

We completed eating our lunch, and after a choice of cherry or apple pie, we cleaned away the dishes and just sat around the table.

I told Bruce and La Dawn that we had started a Christmas tradition and would like to make them a part of it. I said that during the Christmas season, I had several people contribute in many different ways. I mentioned the help of the dentist, funds contributed, ladies helping to sew Santa suits, donated toys by a toy shop owner, etc. I told them that I had made them a very select group of people: honorary elves. "And now it is my honor to make you honorary Santa's Elves." I handed them the plaque.

You never know what type of reaction you'll get in a situation like this, and I could never have anticipated their response. They both first held the plaque together and admired it, and then, as though we were not even there, they ran around the house trying to find the perfect place to hang it. Once they found the spot, right next to a collage of family pictures—an honored spot,

Bruce ran and got a hammer and a nail and it was hung in its rightful place.

Then they sat on the sofa, stared at it, and started to shed a few tears. To them, their goodness had been validated. Sometimes you just need someone else to tell you that you have "done good," and it just confirms that you are on the right track in life. It is just nice that someone has noticed.

The thought came to me that, as Santa, I should be more aware of the good that people do and be free with my praises to them. I thought back to the mall at Christmas and the young man who helped an older lady carry her packages to her car. When he returned, I should have gotten out of my Santa "throne," walked right over to him, and let him know how impressed I was.

After a good conversation and a pledge from them to help out anyway they could in the future, we said our goodbyes and left with the knowledge that they and we had both been blessed.

As we drove away, Sarah said, "I think from now on I would like to go on all your visits with you."

We arrived home a little after 3 p.m., plenty of time for Sarah to make a refreshment for game night with Ann and Mable. Because I had offered my help, I renewed my offer and was told she had plenty of time.

She told me that cooking time was thinking time; it was a good time for her to just ponder life. She said, "It will give me time to think of our visit today. I kind of want to give it a place in my heart.

# 14

## Call to Elfdom

I called a catering company we had used often in the old company I had worked for. I asked for Mattie. She had helped me plan and execute many company affairs with much success.

When Mattie came on the line, she recognized my voice immediately and said, "Robert, tell me you're not going to plan a bankruptcy party."

After a good laugh, I told her that it was about as bad because I wanted her to cater a Christmas dinner with all the trimmings.

She said, "Is this for next Christmas already?"

I said, "No this is for last Christmas."

When I told her about the situation of the company's never having a Christmas party, she grabbed the idea like it was her own. "Fortunately we haven't as yet put all our Christmas paraphernalia away, so we'll just drag it out," she said; "this was a particularly festive year."

I gave her all the details, asked her if she could arrange for Christmas music to be playing, and was told not to worry about a thing.

She asked to whom she should send the bill, and I told her Santa, and gave her my address. I told her also that I might need her for some future occasions.

She said, "Wait a minute. Did you say *Santa*?"

I laughed and said, "That's who I am now. I'll explain later."

She said, "We are always looking for a good Santa. Can I call you later to just see what you're up to?"

I told her to call me anytime.

I don't know what Sarah was cooking, but the smell of it pulled me from my desk and toward the kitchen. She met me at the door but wouldn't let me in. I again asked her what she was cooking, and she said it was a surprise—Ann and Mable's favorite. I said it smells like it could be mine also.

We freshened up a little, and it wasn't too long before the doorbell rang and we greeted Mable and Ann. They always brought more than themselves; they were so pleasant to be around; they never came in but what the house seemed to fill with good feelings.

I can't remember when we started to become such good friends. We had lived in the same neighborhood for more than thirty years. It had been comfortable all those years to know there were people around you could rely on in times of need, small or large. I don't know how many cups of sugar we had exchanged over those years. Their jovial nature always made their visits welcome. I never knew what they would come up with.

Mable said, "I swear, Robert, I think you're losing weight. It would be easier for you to eat than for us to have to alter your Santa suit."

I ushered them into the living room and positioned them together on the sofa. They both looked a little surprised.

Mable said, "Aren't we going into the game room, or are you tired of being beaten all the time?" She gave a little giggle.

Sarah came in and took her place in one of the armed chairs. When she sat down, I'll never know why but everything became very quiet. All three of them looked at me as though they were looking for an explanation.

I said, "I have something I want to talk to you about. I'll still beat you at the game later, but I thought this was important enough to spend some formal time on it. Anne and Mable looked back and forth at each other.

I continued: "I was talking to Sarah the other day, and she said that you think I should have a second Santa suit. That talk started me to doing some thinking, and I came to the conclusion that you should know exactly what is going on with Santa Claus. You see, I am living a double life. When I'm around you, I'm just plain old Robert. But when we're not together, I am someone else."

Ann said, "Well, there's never been anything plain about the Robert I know."

Mable added, "Maybe homely but never plain."

After a little giggle from the three ladies, I went on: "This may be hard for you to imagine, but after Christmas and all the fun we had, Sarah and I decided that I should be a full-time Santa, and by full time I mean a real Santa Claus, a year-around Santa."

Mable turned to Ann and said, "See I told you there was a reason that he hasn't shaved his beard off."

I went on to tell them that I wouldn't be building a toy factory and train reindeer how to fly, but I could be real in many ways. I went on to tell them about some of the meaningful things that happened to us at Christmas time and several times since. As stories were revealed, tears came to their eyes.

I said, "To all of those people we helped, I was a very real Santa Claus. I in fact had a physical existence where they were concerned. They didn't have to imagine me up; I was there for them, and they could tell real rather than fictitious stories about me."

I continued, "As you know, a lot of folks helped out to make our first year a very great Christmas, and I made several of them honorary elves, but I think, and Sarah agrees, that in order for Santa to become even more real, he has to have real, not just honorary, elves. I have been given quite a large sum of money with a promise of more if it is needed. We believe we can make people very happy and can even do it all year round."

Ann said, "I think what you have done is nothing short of a miracle. And to think that we had just a little bit to do with it.

I can tell you it just makes me feel good all over." Mable

added, "We're still here to help, you know. Don't count us out if you need something done."

I said, "That is just it. We don't want to count you out; we want to count you in. In fact, we are asking you to be our real elves—not just honorary ones."

Things went silent for about one minute as I let it sink in. Mable and Ann turned to each other and took each other's hands, saying nothing, but nodding their heads to each other in a positive way.

Needless to say, Sarah was not going to be left out of this. She ran over and wiggled her way in between them, and the three hugged each other. Tears were in order, and I threw them a tissue box that I had anticipated they would be needing.

Mable broke up the excitement by saying, "But I don't even know what an elf is or is supposed to do."

I said, "Well before I started, do you think I knew what a Santa was supposed to do?"

Ann added, "Well I don't suppose that it would be too hard. Do we have to wear elf clothes?"

I said, "I thought you already did. Just look at the two of you— polka dots and stripes. What you always wear will do just fine." And then I said, "Can I be very serious for just a minute?" Their reaction to this request was one of the reasons they were chosen.

Ann said, "Are elves supposed to be serious? It seems to me that all the elves I've ever seen were always playing but even when working were having fun."

I answered: "And this is the way I want it to be. Our jobs should never be so solemn that we can't enjoy them. I've never met the real Santa or even seen a real elf. In fact, I think that's the way it's supposed to be. Most of the things we have to do should be done from the background. I started writing lists of things we can do, even a mission statement to say why we do what we do, but I felt it best if we just play it by ear and learn from each other just what a Santa and his Elves should be doing."

"I don't want to say that this is an experiment because it's not. The fact is that we will have to take what we have, which in both of your cases is quite a lot, and develop the skills needed through involvement, practice, and knowledge to make us a very proficient team. In reality, I don't think your lives will have to change very much. You will just have to be more aware of elf opportunities, and I believe we should be equal in the calling. All suggestions and, yes, even criticisms will be appreciated.

"I'd rather that you not give me your answer tonight. I would like you to take some time to think how this will fit into your lives. You should know that there are not any financial rewards for doing this work, but you will be reimbursed in so many other ways—in ways that make life worth living.

"I believe that all of these years we have known each other have merely been years of preparation. We have lived together and helped each other through all sorts of times. Our love for each other has been proven. We have given to each other over and over again and know the blessings of having someone around you who cares. Now, we together can expand that love and care to others, and with a joint effort, we can influence many lives. I sincerely believe that we will make a great team. We have all been given incredible lives, and now it is time to give our lives to others."

I knew what their answer would be. The tears in their eyes bespoke their nature. Not only would they answer to the call but they would also go far beyond what they were asked to do.

Some may think that I might have been asking too much of these ladies who were getting on in life. My view was somewhat different. To me, getting on in life meant you should be getting on with life. What does age have to do with what you can and cannot accomplish? All age means is that you have to do what needs to be done in a different manner. If working would be hard on them and hurry up the death process, what would be wrong with that? A full, short life is much better than a long, empty life.

Older people should not be told to take life easy now, to sit back and enjoy what you have accomplished, and to slow down.

They should be told to hurry up. After all, there isn't much life left. With a full life of learning and experience, they should be prepared to offer more now than ever. One of the greatest mistakes young people make is that of not taking advantage of those who have already lived what they must look forward to living themselves.

Questions kept coming up while we were playing our games. With them somewhat distracted, I even won one game.

Ann asked, "How do we actually become real elves? Do we just change from who we are and one day become an elf?"

I assured her that it was about that easy. "One day I just became Santa." I knew she needed more information, and added, "Remember the one day you just became a mother? The day before you weren't. Well, it is much like that. You take on new responsibilities; you feel totally devoted to your baby; but you are the same person. Your life isn't your own anymore because it is shared. You do nothing without determining not only how you will be affected but also how the other person in your life will be influenced. Being an elf is like this. You become more concerned with those around you than you do with yourself. That is why I said it wouldn't be a big change for you or Mable. You both already do more for others than you do for yourselves."

Sarah brought in the dessert, and said, "To give you a little kick start, I made your favorite dessert. This should sweeten things up a little."

She gave us each a generous portion of crème brûlée. It was a great finish for the night.

We left with an understanding that we would both give this the amount of thought it deserved and would meet again in one week. I didn't think they would need this much time but wanted them to ponder the significance of what they were about to do. A quick decision usually leads to a weaker resolve. Because of the unreal nature of what we were about to do, we needed real devotion. If we didn't believe in ourselves, no one else would.

# 15

## *Kate, Our New Mall Elf*

The one thing I hate about bad news is that it usually can't be changed. I went right to the lab when I arrived at the hospital the next morning and was told that my kidney was not a match for Martin Burgess.

I went to give him the news only to find out he had already been told. He seemed to be in good spirits and said that as old as I was, my kidney may not have lasted too long anyway. They still had hope and would know within the hour of another donor who they said was universal.

Martin said, "Can we just talk about Christmas?"

I told him I would love to.

He said, "First the bad news. We won't have Haley again. She has been accepted into some big music school in New York City, so we both should be on the lookout for a replacement elf."

I immediately thought of Ann and Mable but couldn't quite see them flitting around the mall. I would make an effort to go to more concerts and plays—anywhere talent would be displayed to find my Christmas elf. I was kind of leaning toward a singing elf this year.

Martin told me that management had increased his budget for the coming Christmas season. "They are pushing me to get an extended contract with you for the season, so we will be able to increase your pay and still have plenty left to refurbish our Santa scene and add a few new improvements. Our last management meeting was almost all on the subject of Christmas, and there were a lot of great ideas thrown around."

Whether it was fate or just plain luck, while we were talking, a young girl dressed in a candy striper uniform, a youth voluntary group, came into the room carrying a nice bouquet of roses someone had sent Martin. She looked around the room that was totally filled with other flowers from well-wishers and said to Martin, "You must be a great guy to be so loved."

She asked if she could bring the flowers in and arrange them for him. She took the time to place them in a perfect spot and said, "I'll be right back."

She left, but it wasn't even a few moments before she returned. She had a large watering can and went around the room filling each flower vase with the proper amount of water. She was humming a little tune as she went around, and I was totally captivated.

I turned to her and asked, "You wouldn't happen to be a singer, would you? I mean, do you like to sing?"

She said, "I'd sing right out loud all the time if it were proper. I love to sing."

It was more than I could hope for. Here was a girl who had volunteered her time to help people, she loved to sing, and she was as friendly as could be.

Martin soon saw what I was getting at, and picked up on my excitement. He asked her age, if she were in school, and if she lived nearby. He asked about her parents. She didn't seem to mind the questions because she had already determined, in her mind, that we were nice-enough guys.

After answering the questions, she asked one of her own, "Why do you want to know all of these things?"

Martin turned to me and said, "Do you want to tell her?"

I said, "You're doing fine, go ahead."

Martin went on, "Well, I guess we should introduce ourselves first. This wonderful fellow here is Santa Claus—the real one."

She looked a little startled, but a guarded smile on her face confirmed that she was willing to consider this.

Martin went on, "I'm Martin Burgess, one of the managers of the Downtown Mall, and we are looking for an elf to help Santa this coming Christmas season. We just thought you might make a wonderful elf, and that would give you the chance to just sing out whenever you wanted to."

To our surprise, she said excitedly, "I saw you as Santa last year and loved your elf. She played a flute, didn't she?"

I said, "Her name was Haley, and she was a great elf."

She then said, "I said to myself that I would someday like to do that. It looked like the two of you were having so much fun."

Thoughts and questions were presenting themselves in my head, and they needed addressing to make this miracle happen. I think both Martin and I, without so much as a nod of the head, agreed that we had found our girl. How it had happened so fast was probably bouncing around in both of our heads. It seemed like almost too much of a coincidence; it all seemed that it had somehow been previously arranged.

I still didn't know how good of a singer she was. I had heard her humming, and it was pleasant. Could she just by chance have a loving, caressing, expressive voice? She was probably still in high school. How could she take the time to be an elf?

When I approached her with the high school question, she said, "Oh! That won't be a problem, I finished all of my requirements for graduation last year, and I am taking college-credit courses now. My time is virtually my own."

As though she were reading our minds and wanted to put us totally at rest, she said, "If you want to hear me sing, our school is putting on the musical *Carousel*; and I just happen to have the lead role. Performances start in two weeks. I'll make sure you get good tickets."

She looked at Martin and said tenderly, "I guess you won't be able to come by then." And then she cheered up and said, "Well, we are filming it, and I'll see that you get a DVD!

She went on, "Oh, I'd love to be your elf. Of course, I would have to discuss it with my parents before I could say yes, and I'm sure there's more you'll want to know about me. Oh, by the way, my name is Kate."

She took a pen from Martin's table and wrote her name, address, and phone number and where the musical would be held. She was thorough. She said she was on duty and there was still a lot she had to get done. "But please call me." And then she left.

Martin didn't even stop to talk about what had just happened. He said, "We'll build her a little stage that will have a spotlight, and we'll have accompaniment for all the Christmas songs recorded. Any song she wants to sing she'll just have to push a button, the lights will reflect the mood, and the music will begin. And we'll set up a microphone and have a good sound system for her."

# 16

## Martin's Good News

There was no news that day about a matching donor, but none of us seemed to be concerned. Each of us seemed to have a certainty or confidence that a donor would be found, and that thinking gave us a buoyancy to move on to the next day.

It started snowing on the way home, and I decided not to take the freeway home. As the storm got rather severe, I started thinking what might happen if my Buick couldn't make it through the deep snow. I thought a four-wheel-drive might be the answer. I did make it home but just barely.

On my own street I had to stop and help a neighbor get unstuck so I could get around him. Sarah was looking out the front window when I drove up; she always seemed to worry when a storm started. She met me at the door and helped me with my scarf and coat and told me I should have worn my boots.

It was still quite early in the day, and I said, "Let's just go sit in front of the fireplace, and I'll bring you up to date on everything that has happened. We'll have a Santa and Mrs. Santa meeting."

She went into the kitchen while I got the fire going and came back with two cups of hot chocolate with little marshmallows in mine. There was never any room between us as we sat on the couch. Sarah loved to cuddle and was just the right size to make it fun.

I brought her up to date on what was happening to Martin. I couldn't donate a kidney, but they might have found him one.

He would be going home on Sunday, and if a replacement kidney was not found in a week, they would start dialysis.

I told her that we had an informal Christmas planning meeting, and that Martin told me Haley wouldn't be available to be my elf this year.

"And then the oddest thing happened," I said. "A young girl who was a voluntary candy striper who just went around helping people, not ten minutes after Martin had told me about Haley, walked into Martin's room with a bouquet of flowers. She was perfect in every way and must have a beautiful singing voice because she's singing the lead in her school musical. Well, to make a long story short, she is not only available but is very excited about being our elf."

Sarah sat forward on the couch and almost to herself said, "There is much more to this than meets the eye. This has to be fate; there has to be some force or principle or even power that predetermined this would happen."

I told her that we had to get parental permission, but Kate said she was sure her parents wouldn't object. The subject of another elf costume came up, and Sarah got very enthusiastic to say the least.

Most of Saturday was spent shoveling snow from the front walk and the driveway and then going to Ann and Mable's to make sure they were all right.

On Sunday, right after church, our phone rang, and I was surprised to hear Martin's voice. He seemed excited and told me that they had found him a kidney and that the operation would be Monday afternoon.

He said, "I'm not going home; I'll just stay here and they will prep me for the operation." He quieted down a bit and asked if I might be able to come in Monday morning and say another prayer before he went in for the surgery.

I had always been religious by nature, but as I grew older, I became religious by experience. I loved the scriptures, and reading them daily had become a habit. By reading the good book, I had come to have an understanding of God, and communing with Him came naturally. I felt honored that Martin would consider me a man of faith, and I told him I would be there for him.

# 17

## New Cars for Old

It didn't seem to be difficult. In fact, I felt that everything was made easier because of my belief in a superior being. Of course I thought it was important that I believe, but I also thought it was important that other aspects of my life received equal time, including the mental and social. I always thought that the world was so well organized and balanced, that to retain a state of equilibrium a person must also seek his own balance to enjoy what was around him.

I believed that as in religion, the highest standards must be pursued in all of our endeavors. In one of our meetings one of our church leaders was teaching this principle. He said we should search after anything that was lovely or of good report. Yes, we should read the scriptures, but there are many offerings that could enhance a man's life. He went on to teach that a true mark of an intelligent man is to know what *not* to read.

The same is true about music and movies; in fact, it's true about everything a man chooses to share his time with, even the people with whom he closely associates. Yet I believe that a person should associate with everyone. There are those he can learn from and those he can teach. You can go out on a limb—but only if you have great balance.

As I arrived at church on Sunday, our leader, who was called our "bishop," pulled me aside. I had told him earlier to let me know if anyone needed any kind of help. He told me that the church had helped Diane Winters, a member of the congregation, to complete her college education. She had lost her husband about a year and a half ago and was determined to raise her three children the best she could by herself. She was just offered a job that was perfect for her situation. She could drop her children off at school each morning on her way to work.

She had a pretty decent vehicle that one of the other church members, a mechanic, keeps in good condition for her, but the tires were bald and dangerous.

He took me out to the parking lot and showed me the vehicle. I didn't even trust her to drive home on those tires, and the vehicle itself looked like it was of a vintage where it might not be road worthy for too much longer.

I told him I would take care of it and wrote the tire size down. There was nothing I could do until Monday morning. I got her address from the bishop.

While sitting in church, where you are usually prompted to do what's good, a plan came into my mind, one that I would have to act on almost immediately. After the closing prayer, I worked my way through the members to where Diane was sitting.

I knew Diane well and loved her. I sat next to her and asked, "Do you have any personal belongings you need to take out of your car?"

She said, "No, just the title and insurance papers."

She looked at me quizzically, but before she could ask any questions, I said, "I have a proposition to make you. I have to get rid of my car and was wondering if you would just like to trade vehicles?" I held out my keys and asked for hers in return. She asked if I was serious, stated that my car was worth much more than hers, and pointed out that right now she couldn't pay the difference.

I assured her that it would be an even trade.

Her only reply was, "I have often admired your car when I've seen you pull up."

And then I said, "Then it's a deal." I took my house keys off the key fob and handed her the keys.

She said, "You mean we're going to do this right now?"

I said, "Only if you'll give me your car, I have to get home some way." The exchange was made, I also had to throw in a handkerchief to close the deal.

I went back to pick up Sarah. She seemed to always be the last one out of the building because she so liked to talk to everyone. I simply said, "Let's go home, Sweetheart."

Just as we stepped into the parking lot our Buick drove by, gave a honk, and Diane and her kids waved at us.

Sarah said, "Isn't that our car?"

I said, "Not any longer," and I pointed to Diane's car and said, "That's ours now." I opened the passenger door and Sarah slid in, looking a little surprised. Before closing the door, I said, "I'll tell you about it on the way home."

I loved Sarah's reaction. She just sat there as though this was something we do on a weekly basis. When I explained the situation to her, her only remarks were, "Well, we couldn't let them drive around on poor tires."

I told her that those were my exact sentiments because if anything happened to them, I would feel awful. I then told her about my experience of driving in the snow and how I thought of getting a four-wheel-drive vehicle. I could use Diane's car for a trade in, and we could take a little out of our savings account to cover the rest.

I apologized for making such a quick decision without talking it over, and she just cozied up a little closer to me as the heater in the car was not a very good one. The only comment she made was, "I always felt a little uppity in that car anyway." So the car trade was a done deal. We took much longer to get home that day, as we drove very slowly on bad tires.

We started to find that all the things we had bought and thought we really needed were nowhere near as important as the needs of others. If people can give abundantly, they should. And if they don't have the means, they should give at least something anyway.

# 18

## A Prayer for Martin

My first call Monday morning was at the hospital. As I walked into Martin's room, his daughter and someone whom I thought was probably his wife were sitting in his room.

"Hi Santa!" his daughter said, and then introduced me to her mother, who was a sophisticated but uncomplicated lady—one whom you would desire as a friend the first time you met her. The lines at the corners of her mouth and eyes were kind, not developed by a harshness, but reflective of a propensity to smile. She was lovable—someone you just wanted to hug. And so I did.

Her daughter told her that she was sitting in my chair, and I said, "No wife trumps Santa." I leaned over and gave Martin a hug around his shoulders as it just seemed the natural thing to do. Our relationship had advanced. What was once a handshake had now progressed to a hug, a higher form of affection. *What seems natural to do, should be done*, I thought to myself.

Martin thanked me for coming, and said very happily that everything was still a "go."

What a marvelous world! Our friendship, and his wife and daughter's love, could be extended for many years because others tried to solve some of the trials of life—and succeeded. I told Martin I was thankful that I could have him as a friend and that our time together could be so much longer.

I wiped beginning tears away and, turning to Martin's wife and daughter said, "I guess Martin told you that he asked me to come and say a prayer before he goes into surgery. I just want you to know that, to me, to be asked to do this is a great honor. He has deemed me as someone who is close to God, and I can think of no greater compliment. I want you to know that I believe with all my heart in God and His goodness. I also believe He has the ability to direct the affairs of men and women.

"He is most likely to bless those who have faith in Him, and Martin's asking for a prayer is definitely an indication of his faith. When I pray for Martin, I become the spokesperson for him and for you. I will express your desires and ask God to fulfill them for you. The Bible tells us that God is the same yesterday, today, and forever. He is perfect, and what He does cannot be improved on.

"He loves us as much today as He did the prophets and the people in the days of Christ. If God's Son came to earth and healed people and gave them blessings, it was because He loved them. He loves us equally; he will not withhold blessings from us. He said all we have to do is ask, and that is what we will do in our prayer—we will ask. A man as good as Martin will receive the blessings he asks for. If you don't mind, can we kneel around Martin's bed together, and be joined in this prayer."

I stepped out of the room for just a moment and let the nurse know we would like some privacy for just a few minutes. And then I went back in and kneeled together with them.

It was obvious to all of us that the Spirit had attended us. Words were said that were given us to say—too sacred to be rehearsed here, but each of us had a certainty of God's love and assurance that everything would go satisfactorily. We don't have experiences too often like this in our lives, but just leave it to say that we should remember the spirit more than the words.

I left my phone number with Martin's wife, got my second round of hugs, and left Martin in a very agreeable mood.

# 19

## *Santa's New Sleigh*

I got in my old car and drove to the dealership I had been doing business with for years. Doug always stopped what he was doing and gave me his whole attention. He said, "I can't believe what I just saw you drive up in; what did you do with the Buick?"

I told him the story and said that I would be driving much more in the snow and needed a reliable four-wheel-drive.

He said, "You just gave the Buick away?" and slipped into deep thought longer than a very talkative man usually does. He went on to tell me that I had been a good customer for many years and that maybe they could be a little more generous in helping me out with a new vehicle.

I said, "That would be helpful inasmuch as I don't have a job anymore."

He said, "Oh yes, I heard about your company."

Doug asked me what kind of four-wheel-drive I had in mind, and I told him I had always been partial to the Jeep Grand Cherokee. He said, "You're in luck; I just took a two-year-old very low miles and very clean Jeep Grand Cherokee in on trade. There is only one problem. It is red—a very pretty red, but nonetheless red."

I thought for a minute, and concluded that red was the exact color Santa should have and told him that it was exactly what I was looking for. That kind of startled him. I had played down wild colors in all the cars I had bought in the past.

He worked me up "a deal I couldn't refuse," only this time it was much better than I could have ever expected. He gave me much more than the old car was worth and sold me the Jeep much lower than book value. I drove out with a beautiful, red Jeep Grand Cherokee. I purposely drove through several snow banks on the way home just for the fun of it. He told me to send Diana in as soon as possible, and they would take care of all the titling, registration, and licensing for me.

Sarah was a little surprised but loved the Jeep and said, "Just a minute." She ran into the house, and it wasn't but a very short time later that she came running out with her coat and wanted to go for a ride. She said, "Maybe we could get into the mountains more this summer; you know how you love to fish."

Somehow, I had a hard time picturing Santa fly fishing on a stream. The thought of fish brought us to the decision to stop for lunch at a little restaurant that served English-style fish and chips—cod deep fried in a batter that enhanced its taste to perfection, and French fries with malt vinegar sprinkled on them. It was a perfect combination.

We would pass the hospital on the way home, and I thought it a perfect time for Sarah to meet Martin. I pulled into the parking lot and said, "Come on, let's go see how Martin's surgery went."

Sarah looked down at herself as a self-inspection to see if she would pass Martin's scrutiny. She said what I thought she would say: "Well, I didn't exactly dress for the occasion."

I thought about that comment and told her she always looks great. I can't remember a time in our lives that I haven't been very proud of my wife.

Martin had just been brought out of the recovery room, and Sarah said, "Maybe we had better come back a little later."

I saw Martin's wife busily pulling the covers over Martin and straightening his pillows. She saw us in the hall and said, "Santa, please come in, and this must be your wife." She introduced herself to Sarah, "I'm Jean, Martin's wife." She went on to tell us that the doctors were very pleased with the operation. "Everything went perfectly and is functioning the way it should, and Martin could probably come home in less than a week."

Our happiness and relief were evident to her, and she said, "You have been such a good friend."

"We just wanted to make sure everything went perfectly, and good friends know that the best hospital visit is a short visit. We'll check in periodically, but if you need us for any reason, just call," I said.

When we got to the Jeep Sarah said, "Well there's one thing for sure: Martin is in good hands."

# 20

## Committed Elves

When we arrived home we checked our phone for any messages and had one from Mable. She said, "Hi, this is Mable. Ann and I have come to a decision but just can't wait until Thursday night to tell you. Could we come over tonight?"

I told Sarah to give them a call and invite them over; I couldn't wait either.

Ann and Mable came over shortly after dinner, walked right in the front door, went directly to the living room, and took their appointed places. It looked like they had determined that Ann would be their spokesperson. I asked them if they had come to a decision.

Ann said, "If you're asking us if we've made our minds up, the answer is yes. If you ask us if we are determined, it is a definite yes. If you ask us if we know what we are doing, the answer is no."

I said, "I think you do know what you're doing. I'm sure you don't know everything you are supposed to be doing, but I'm also sure you know some of the things elves are asked to do. But first, is your answer Yes, you will be my elves?"

Mable said, "We would love to."

I let them know that as far as I knew, we were pretty well equal in what we do. I could ask them to do certain jobs, but they could also ask me in turn to help them when they needed me.

I said, "Your abilities to be elves will be increased, and you will be surprised by the changes that take place in your lives. I once heard that elves, because of their loving countenances, were called divinities of light or aelfen. That means they're 'God -like.' Santa has been called a jolly old elf, so we are all to be elves together. I think all we have to do to become productive elves is to develop the divinities we have within ourselves—or to be like God. You will find that you will have increased perceptive powers to comprehend and be more aware of others' needs."

Mable commented, "It sounds almost mystical, doesn't it."

"It is mystical." I replied. "Do you know any other elves?"

Ann asked, "What do we do first?"

I replied, "Now that you mention it, I think your idea for a second Santa suit is great. Maybe we could make another one." I thought it important to let them know they had a choice in all we did. And if they chose not to do it, that was all right. I then told them about Haley and the fact that we would probably need a new elf outfit when we found the right girl to replace her. I told them that we had a good prospect, that her name is Kate, and that we would like to invite them to go with Sarah and me to her Carousel performance. They were delighted.

Ann, always the one who insisted upon "dotting the i's and crossing the t's," said, "Is that it, then? Are we now elves, or do we have to be officially appointed?"

As I had anticipated, some sort of a ceremony would be needed to make it legitimate. I told them we ought to have a swearing-in ceremony to make it official. They seemed very pleased, and together we decided that Thursday night would be appropriate. We then determined that from now on, a portion of our Thursday nights would be a Christmas business meeting.

Needless to say, as the night went on, they had more questions than I had answers. We had a lot of laughs at our naivety, but the serious moments, while we considered our purposes and what responsibilities we had actually assigned to ourselves, gave us moments to consider the significance of what we were about to do.

Sarah put a fitting end to the night by stating, "Oh thank you, Ann and Mable. You have always been an inspiration to us, and now you can inspire so many others with your many talents and love."

Hugs went around the room. I was soon to find out that this would be the most cuddling, squeezing, embracing bunch of elves ever assembled. I didn't mind it. I was always taught that a hug was just a roundabout way of expressing yourself. We welcomed and parted with a hug, we showed support with a hug, but, best of all, we experienced acceptance with each hug.

# 21

## *The Art of Giving Gifts*

I went again to the hospital the next morning. This would probably be my last visit to Martin before he was released to go home. He was alone and looked great. I was surprised at how quick his recovery was.

After a health check and a short meeting for the coming Christmas, he said, "Kate stopped by and left me some tickets for her performance. There are four tickets, but we will not be able to attend. So you can find someone to go with you. Kate said that she had her parents' approval, and they of course would like to know the conditions of her working for us."

I told Martin to keep me updated on his progress, and he said, "As soon as I am back to work I'll call and we'll get together." We bid our farewells.

I had four or five hours with nothing planned, so I thought this might be a good time to pick a subject I wanted to know more about and begin my studies on how to be Santa.

I opened my new journal to the back, and out of the many subjects I had listed, I chose giving. I chose this subject because it is the essence of Christmas. The pleasurable anticipation of being on the receiving end of a gift is what intensifies and heightens the excitement of the Christmas season. When we are favorably stimulated by the hope of obtaining items we deem very desirable, our whole being is awakened, and this arousal adds great degrees of happiness to our lives.

I knew that you couldn't give unless you first possessed something. So in my own mind, I came up with the following understanding: *Giving is passing on something you own to somebody without expecting compensation for it, and, in all cases, it has to be given voluntarily.*

There were so many questions I had about giving that I decided to start listing them and adding to them as others popped up. I had to be an expert on giving. Most of the questions were fun, but some were very concerning:

1. *What gift would please me the most?*
2. *Who is or was my favorite gift giver so far in life?*
3. *What was the most expensive gift ever given me, and how did it affect me?*
4. *What makes a gift appropriate?*
5. *What is the best manner to give a gift?*
6. *Have I ever given a gift grudgingly or out of compulsion?*
7. *What if you don't have anything to give?*
8. *Why do human beings give?*

I'm sure that as I studied these questions, other questions would present themselves. This is just a place to start. I am very sure that there is not a person living who doesn't have something to give. Thus, everyone should be a giver. It is evident to me that money should not determine whether a gift should be given or not, and to be classified as a giver, you don't have to give to everyone. All you have to do is to give to one person.

It's also evident to me that the more you give, the better you will understand giving. I have often thanked the Lord that I could give instead of depending on others to give to me.

The first question came up because it seems to me that we will probably never be given that which we want the most. After going through my mind, I remembered several desired gifts—like a new pair of waders for fly fishing, a very expensive collection of a series of church books that includes 30 books, an iPad, and several other lesser items. I settled on the iPad. The iPad I wanted would cost $477. So I thought, *What are the chances someone might give me one? How long would I have to wait? Why do I really want one? And is it something I can give myself?*

The only person I could think who would get me one would be Sarah, and because she probably couldn't trust herself when it came to buying high-tech electronics, this would probably never happen. I really didn't need one anyway. I had managed to get through 65 years without one, and if I really talked myself into how much easier it would make my life, I could buy one anyway. It was certain that if anyone asked me what I wanted for Christmas, I wouldn't tell them an iPad.

I once asked one of my sons what he wanted for Christmas. Children will tell you exactly what they want; cost or availability or even room to house it doesn't matter. He told me he wanted a horse. When I asked him where we would keep it, he said, "In the back yard." I asked him how we would feed it, and he said, "All they eat is hay!" He had thought it through thoroughly and had all the answers. My only thought was, *How disappointed will he be Christmas morning when there is no horse under the tree?*

I came to the conclusion that the wants of a person should very rarely determine the gift given. A gift addressing the needs of a person will in almost all cases be more appropriate. On some occasions, the receivers might not even know of a need they have.

In all cases, I found that going shopping without a gift in mind will usually not result in a proper gift. If I know the person and consider her or him worthy of a gift, I should know well enough after an analysis to know what to give. It may take some thought to determine the appropriate gift, but a gift should never be given where the person receiving it is not given the respect or the consideration deserved.

If a person doesn't want to be disappointed in life, that person shouldn't build up a want list. I thought of even starting by asking those I intended to give to, "What do you *need* for Christmas—instead of what do you *want*?" I was sure I'd be surprised at how my gift list would change and at how pleased most people will be with the gift given them.

When I consider who my favorite giver was, I would have to list my Aunt Clara. We always opened her presents last and always tried to guess what she made us that year. Needless to say, Aunt Clara was not a wealthy aunt, and everything she gave us was homemade. She always made all of us the same thing, so the first one to open her present was the only one to be surprised. Over the years, we had accumulated pajamas, several knitted hats, scarves, and gloves.

On one special Christmas, we had all received what she called toe warmers. They fit over your toes, and, after five seconds in the microwave, they took the chill off your feet.

These gifts kept coming into adulthood. I was always amazed that she would never forget us year after year. I wondered about a lot of things. I wondered how long it had actually taken to make all of these gifts, and I wondered how she decided on what gift to give us. But I never wondered if she loved us. In this case, we appreciated the giver more than the gift.

I hadn't received too many expensive gifts in my lifetime. It may have been because my family wasn't too well to do, and we certainly didn't have any rich friends or relatives.

But, on one occasion, my parents gave me a Wollensak reel-to-reel tape recorder. It was considered, at that time, to be the best recorder that was offered. It completely surprised me because I hadn't ever made a request for such an item. My parents knew I liked to sing and thought it would be fun for me to record some of the songs I sang. I enjoyed it for about the first week, but there wasn't much to do with it other than record my own voice, which I soon tired of hearing. It didn't sound like me anyway. I soon ran out of tapes, the earphones burned out, and cost prohibited my getting new ones. So the expensive Wollensak sat unused for years until, when I moved out, it was discarded for lack of use and old age.

Over the years, I had felt good that my parents had given me something they thought would be good for me, but I always felt guilty that I hadn't put it to better use. I learned in time that it is not the cost of the gift but the use of the gift that gives it value. Give me something that will last a long time; this makes the gift immortal and always refreshes my memory of the giver.

_Appropriateness_ seems to me to be the operative word when it comes to giving gifts. The right gift given at the right time, to the right person, for the right reason, is the perfect gift. There is nothing more fulfilling than giving the perfect gift.

I thought, _Is there one gift that is appropriate for all people?_ The answer was a resounding _Yes!_, but before I could give it, I would have to get it. The answer, of course, is love, the perfect gift. So, to me, the answer was easy. Why give a gift if you don't love someone? And if you still want to give a gift, find a reason to love the person—and then find the suitable gift that lets the person know this.

It is important for me to realize that I came into this world with all the love needed. If I once had it and lost it, it is easy to find again. There is not a person living who doesn't deserve my love. There are those who don't recognize love when it is given. You say to yourself, _I know what I have given. They just don't recognize what they have been given. It doesn't matter, I have given the right gift for the right reason. The fact that they don't understand this does not diminish me or the gift given. My actions were appropriate._ Isn't that what's important—that we determine what is right and do it? I came to the conclusion that no gift is the right gift if love isn't involved. No gift is inappropriate if love is involved.

We have been told that the manner of giving is worth more than the gift. I determined from this thought that I should take more time considering how to present the gift.

For example, I just can't seem to wrap a present profession- ally. I can't match edges, and the paper seems to get all wrinkly. However, on one occasion, I gave a gift to a person and said, "I'm sorry about the wrapping, but it is the best I've done to date. I thought of having someone wrap it for me but I wanted this gift to be from me in every way. I thought of what to give you. I went and picked it out, and I wrapped it myself. I just wanted everything about it to be from me to say I love you."

The person thought of keeping it forever—still wrapped up, to remember the beautiful sentiment. We've all been given just enough creative ability to know how to tell someone we love him or her.

We've all had the experience of feeling that we have to give someone a gift. It goes something like this: "Well, I know they will give me a gift, so I should probably grab them a little something." Obligation has a duty or a responsibility attached to it. My thought was, *What if I don't comply? After all, there is no legal penalty attached.*

No one likes to feel obligated or forced into any decision. The only law binding us is a moral law. It occurred to me that my involvement in this line of reasoning was in my own self-interest. I probably had not taken enough time to determine why the other person insisted on giving me presents year after year. Maybe I was missing out on a great relationship. I came to the conclusion that self-respect sets our morals, and our manners should be set by respect for others. Do I want to be a person who does what is required or one who goes the extra mile? As the scripture says, "Whosoever shall compel thee to go a mile, go with him twain."

There were times in my life that I literally didn't have enough funds to purchase gifts. The only thing worse than not getting what you want for Christmas is not being able to get a loved one what she or he wants. Many of the greatest gifts given come at such times. Why? Because we have to be inventive. After all, isn't being creative a God-given gift?

When you let your imagination soar, it allows others to be impressed with your ingenious abilities. Many are more impressed with your offering of the mind than with material offerings. Original thoughts, not imitative thinking, will not merely affect the receiver, but she or he will be astounded that you care enough to give it special thought.

All the time I would have spent on shopping could now be spent on being creative. It is a joyful feeling that I can become the creator. So if I am not as imaginative or inspired as others, it doesn't matter. All my receivers have to know is that I took the time necessary to give them a place for thought in my life.

I believe that people are much more imaginative than they believe they are. A few quiet moments where you can think of a person, be it a wife, mother, father, child, grandparents, relatives, good friends, etc., and determine a message you would like them to have and the best way to deliver it will always result in a myriad of blessings—if not for them, at least for you. I thought I might even like to try a Christmas when this is all I do. If you have much, give your wealth; if you have little, give your heart.

When I thought about it, I was very surprised at how many things I have accumulated that I did not receive as a gift from another person. The possessions I enjoy the most I don't even own, yet here they are for me to have every day of my life. These accumulations of wealth have not cost me or anyone else one red cent. No person is richer in these gifts than another; all have them equally.

How meaningful the gifts are to those who receive them depends on how they use them. The appreciation for the gift can be shown only by thanks and love. They are the mountains I can climb or the lake or stream I can fish in. I can lie there and watch the sky's many temperaments. And then there's snow that makes its appearance year after year. The gifts are so numerous that the list would be exhaustive. And as we stop to take a breath, we are given another gift.

I truly believe it is because of the receiving of these gifts that we have an ingrown desire to give. Somewhere in the back of our minds, we know that in our past we had handed to us this great life, and knowing that made us very joyful. It was the ultimate gift. We try to equal this joy in the lives of those we love.

Isn't every gift a way of saying, "I hope this item makes your life better"? Aren't we merely trying to restore what we once felt? A gift is meant to improve a person's life, and the character of the person should be enhanced by the gift. If the gift I give does not spawn love, not so much for the gift but for the giver, have I even given a gift, or am I merely compensating for a lack of companionship?

I loved thinking about a subject until I could come to a conclusion on it. I was told that this is what is called *pondering*. In my research on giving, I came across one statement that pretty well summarized the nature of giving. It came from Elizabeth Bibesco: "Blessed are those who can give without remembering and take without forgetting."

Somewhere I heard it, and I know it is true, that "Every person is guilty of the good he didn't do."

# 22

## *The Elf Ceremony*

I determined that being Santa is a full-time job. That was okay with me because even though there are other things I liked to do, none of them were as satisfying as doing what Santa did. From experience, I knew that if I did all that Santa is supposed to do, I wouldn't have much time left for anything else.

I brought this up with Sarah, thinking that it was okay for me but wanting to make sure it would not cause her any problems.

Her reply was not what I expected to hear, but it was the one I liked to hear. She said, "I'm surprised at you, Robert." She paused for a minute and said, "It is getting harder to call you Robert. Santa just seems more appropriate." She added that she had known me for a long time and always knew that I would never do anything without putting my whole heart into it.

I wouldn't have it any other way.

Then bringing us back to reality, she said, "Are you ready for tonight?"

I had forgotten Mable and Ann were coming over for their "elf ceremony." I had written everything down, but I hadn't printed it out as yet. I started to do the printing and realized my shortcoming in penmanship. Sarah didn't have much success either. I tried laying it out on the computer with several different fonts and was never satisfied with the results. I only had about four hours before they would arrive, and I started to get a little panicky. I had learned a good lesson: no job is so insignificant that it should be put off until the last moment.

I decided to go to my last resort and gave Barbara Barwick a call. I received an answer machine that directed me to her new office number, which when called directed me to her extension.

She answered, "Art Department."

I said, "Is Art there?"

Recognizing my voice she gave a laugh and said, "Robert, how good to hear from you again."

I quickly went through my story of how I had decided to be a full-time Santa.

Her acceptance and excitement were evident through the phone. She said, "You need elf number three to do something for you, don't you?"

I told her I had a one-page document that I needed laid out to present to Mable and Ann because I was raising them from an honorary status to real elves, just like I was being the real Santa.

When she asked when I needed it, I told her in three hours. "That is when I am supposed to make the presentation."

She seemed to pause for a moment, and I knew I just hadn't given her enough time. She said, "I'll do it under one condition, and that is if you will do the same for me." She then just kind of shouted, "I want to be a real elf!"

Very seriously, I said, "Barbara, nothing would make me happier." I had thought of it earlier but didn't know if she could do it along with her work also.

We agreed that I would e-mail the certificate over to her and that she would bring the three documents over in time to take part in the ceremony.

Ann and Mable arrived first. They took their seats but noticed that I had placed a third seat next to theirs. They had known Barbara from previous meetings, and when I told them that she would also serve with us as an elf, they were very excited. The doorbell rang, and Barbara stepped in and fit right in as a hugger.

I had chosen to don my Santa Suit, and when I stepped out, I got a round of applause. Not wanting to make this a formal affair, I decided to sit as we chatted for a moment. Barbara handed me the certificates. Each was rolled into a scroll around a decorated wood dowel that was fastened to the bottom of each document, adding to its authenticity.

I said, "It seems time to get on with the presentation." I then informed them that these meetings held weekly on Thursday nights would be precise and take the form of a business meeting. I asked Ann if she could be our recorder and take notes at each meeting, and then I handed her a hard-backed minute book. I had given this format enough thought to believe that this is how Santa would do it. His house would have to be a house of order, and I was being Santa.

As per the agenda, I told them that I would take any suggestion but had drawn one up until we could add to it or delete unnecessary items. I chose to call it the "Workshop Agenda" because it wasn't just Santa's agenda—it was our agenda.

### WORKSHOP AGENDA
- *Minutes from last meeting*
- *Accounting*
- *Weekly Reporting*
- *Assignments*
- *Business Updates*
- *Discussion*

I told them that because we didn't have a meeting last week, there were no minutes and that we would move right into accounting. I told them that we currently have $33,232 in our account.

Mable was the first to say it: "Where did we get all of that money?"

The explanation took more time than I wanted it to, but I wanted them to know that we were not in this alone. I let them know that all we did for everyone last year came to a little over $2,800. I also reminded them that the $2,800 covered about one month; the $33,232 would be spent throughout the year.

I emphasized to them that we wouldn't be building toys.

However, we would be building girls and boys, and it didn't matter what age they were. Needs have a way of affecting all ages. And some of the needs have costs.

We went through assignments, including the making of a new Santa suit. Barbara had just completed her first assignment, an "Elf Induction Certificate," and we would soon have an elf costume to make. We also had to appear tomorrow night at a high school production of *Carousel*. It was too short of notice for Barbara, so Sarah and I arranged to pick up Mable and Ann in time to get there a little early.

We then had a discussion that could have gone on all night as to what our individual responsibilities were, what our ultimate goals were, and how we expected to accomplish them.

We then got to the ceremony, which I was to lead. I stayed seated but unrolled one of the documents and began reading. They were beautifully done in old English script on parchment paper and in a carmine red-colored ink. They read:

_____ , having all of the attributes necessary to function in the capacity of a full-time elf for Santa Claus, you are duly appointed as such and are given all of the rights, powers, and privileges as pertaining to this appointment.

As an elf, you will be called upon to share your talents and love with every person on the earth.

Dated this ____ day of _____ , in the year of _____ .

Witnessed by:
Santa Claus _____

Each certificate was given in turn, and Barbara, in immaculate handwriting, filled in the names and dates. I then signed each of them.

That I had chosen the right elves would be proven over and over again as the year unfolded.

RICHARD ROBBINS

# 23

## *Kate's Performance*

At the appointed time, Sarah and I picked up Mable and Ann to go see Kate perform in Carousel. Mable and Ann were as giddy as two school girls with the excitement of the occasion.

"I've never been a talent scout before, but mind you I know what I'm doing," Mable said. "I can tell right off if she will be what we're looking for."

Ann said, "When did you get to be so good. You can't sing a lick yourself."

Mable informed us that she had watched every episode of American Idol since its beginning and only on one occasion did she not pick the winner.

We arrived at the auditorium and found our seats, right up front and in the middle. I could tell from the beginning that the school musical director loved what he did. Attention was given to every detail, and we were in for a beautiful night. The school orchestra was even sitting in a pit in front of the stage. We were totally involved from the start.

When Kate first appeared on stage, I pointed her out to my elves. They were enchanted. Sarah gave my hand a little squeeze of approval.

It wasn't until Kate started singing from the first act the song "If I Loved You," that her whole talent was displayed. My three girls had tears, and I could barely see through my own. It wasn't just a performance, it was an accomplishment. By the time she was through we knew what love was and exactly how she felt about it. I could only imagine how wonderful it would be to hear that voice over and over again during the whole Christmas season.

After the performance and several curtain calls the crowd started to disperse. To our surprise Kate came from a side curtain on the stage directly to us. She said, "Did you like it?"

I couldn't get a word in edgewise as Mable and Ann and Sarah gave her the praise she deserved.

She turned to me and said, "What do you think, Santa, will I do as your elf?"

"And then some!" I said. "Your performance was brilliant. I fell in love with you from the start."

I introduced everyone and told her about each of them. "They are real elves, and they do all the work to make Christmas special. They will be the ones to design and sew your special elf costume."

Kate looked at them and stated matter-of-factly, "I kind of figured out who they were before you told me. They have a special glow about them."

Could she have said anything better? I believe their glow increased a little at that time.

Ann took a pen and notebook out of her purse and with the surprised help of Kate started writing down measurements— shoe sizes, height, etc. When she told Kate that they were for her elf costume, Kate said, "Oh can I have one just like last year's elf? It was so darling."

I told Kate that as soon as Mr. Burgess was back at work, we would have a meeting to determine her needs. I told her we had already thought of her own stage or platform with prerecorded instrumentals of all the favorite Christmas songs. "You might want to start making a list of what you want to sing and learn them well."

"My own stage?" Kate said.

"Yes, with your own spotlights and sound system. Your songs will be played throughout the mall," I said.

After our business was over, we said our goodbyes, to which she had to add a hug for each of us. She was special. The ride home was full of laughs and good feelings. I for one had never in my life anticipated Christmas with as much enthusiasm.

# 24

## *Recognizing Needs*

It is amazing how much difference six months can make in a person's life if he or she is determined to change.

I had much to do if I wanted to be Santa. I knew that this would be a lifetime pursuit and was quickly finding out that the more you learned, the more you knew there was to learn and the more you wanted to learn. I learned that all knowledge comes from study, whatever form it takes, whether in reading, research, deep thought, or just observation or experience.

My degree of concentration while engaged in these various activities determined the quantity and quality of my knowledge. In any endeavor that I undertook, I found that knowledge was the key to success. I had hung a sign in my office that says "All knowledge is of itself of some value. There is nothing so minute or inconsiderable that I would not rather know it than not." Those are the words of Samuel Johnson.

I was on my way to being Santa. We—my elves and I—held our weekly meetings and discussed every aspect of Christmas. Because it was getting closer to Christmas, we started a count-down chart to make certain we were covering our bases on all details. Ann came up with a chart that filled our needs and seemed to give us direction.

| Item | Date & Person Assigned | Date to be Completed |
| --- | --- | --- |
| Santa Suit | January 15th, Mable | |
| Elf Costume | February 15th, Mable | |
| Downtown Mall Contract | March 15th, Santa | |
| Booking of Company Parties | August, Santa | November 1st |
| Hospital Visit | September, Santa | December— just before Christmas |
| Token of Appreciation | November 1st, Everyone | Dec. 15th, delivered on Dec. 24th |
| Honorary Elf Plaques | As determined through the year | Delivered Dec. 24th |

There were often occasions that presented themselves that needed Santa's consideration. They came to my attention any number of ways. Many times my elves would say, "Did you see in the news where . . . ?" and then they would go on to describe people with definite needs. These events came up mostly in our weekly meetings during the discussion part of our agenda. Other incidents, as the year went on, came through Santa letters, just meeting people, and even a little gossip. It is amazing what a city will tell you if you listen to it.

Remembering that there is not a person who doesn't have some kind of need led me to a study of how to recognize a need and then how to take care of it.

Needs manifest themselves in as many different variations as there are people, but I learned from studying needs, as part of my Santa studies, that they usually fall into one of several categories:

**1. Physical needs:** I found that these needs are requirements of the body. Without them, human survival would not be possible. Air, water, food, clothing and shelter, and other things pertaining to bodily functions are among physical needs.

To Santa, these needs are easily recognizable and should, in all cases, be given priority. They need immediate attention and are usually easy to attend to. A person cannot function properly if these needs are not met, and other needs will arise if these are not taken care of.

**2. Safety needs:** These needs run the gamut from war, natural disaster, family violence, childhood abuse, economics, health, emergencies, etc. This is a catch-all grouping and seems to include almost all the needs we have. Personal security, financial security, health, and accidents are among the prevalent worries.

Although reactions to when these needs are unmet are more severe, the good thing is that there is usually a solution for them. It may not be immediate, but once recognized, its cure is sure. Usually all it takes to solve these needs is for someone to care. Any need that is not addressed usually magnifies and can cause considerable suffering. The secret is to get the whole community to care. Where there are many willing to help, many needs can be met.

**3. Love and belonging:** Now we start moving into the emotional needs. These are what I came to believe were societal needs. Everyone needs acceptance, a friend, family involvement, and association with others. If not filled properly, these needs can become very dangerous.

People who have such needs often resort to wrong ways to cope with them, such as gang involvement, social drinking, etc., if these are the only outlets they can find. What I found out to be important in these needs is that the person usually has a greater need to love someone than she or he does to be loved. If you can find out what a person's relationship is with those around him or her (family, friends, etc.), you can usually help the person with this need. When a person feels like he or she "fits in" or has a sense of belonging, this secure relationship gives a feeling of ease or acceptance. A proper closeness usually develops into a certain love.

**4.** *Esteem:* Not having a sense of self-worth or having low esteem can cause depression in most people. I have not known a person who does not have a need to feel respected. Even greater than this, I don't know anyone who doesn't need self-respect. Self-respect is only nurtured through adherence to strict guidelines we set for ourselves.

Once self-respect has been obtained, respect from others will be automatic. So all I have to do when I meet a person who does not have inward strength, competence, mastery, confidence, or even independence—each of which is outwardly expressed by an inferiority complex, a weakness, and helplessness—is to let the person know who she or he really is. The greatest good you can give a person is not to convince that person how great you are but how great he or she is. There is not a person living who is not a lot better than the person he or she thinks he or she is.

**5.** *Accomplishment:* When people feel that they have not accomplished everything they possibly could have accomplished, hopelessness can set in. They literally become miserable. This need is recognized by sadness, and even gloominess is felt. Where did the joy of life go?

If a person is still alive, he can still accomplish. He may not be the quarterback of his football team, but he can be the ideal parent or a classical writer or artist. There may have been obstacles, interruptions, or even limitations that deterred such people from an original actualization to express their full potential, but if they can reach their potential now, will it not tell them that they are the people they always thought they were? Our world is full of stories of men and women whose greatest accomplishments came later in life. I have never seen pictures or in my mind visualized Mother Theresa as being a young person.

**6.** *Transcendence:* This is the need we want all people to have. If they have met all their own needs and accomplished all they meant to, they develop a transcendent or superior need. This need can be called a divine need—the need to help others. This need also includes the aesthetic desires we have—the artistic, visual appeal, and the beautiful things of the world. These are the things we stop to admire—the flowers, the composition, and even love. There are those who have as great a need for these transcendent moments as others need shelter and food.

Also, I think it is important to add one more need to the list, and that is the need for fun. To me, this is the ultimate goal. All other goals should be met so this goal can exist. I came to the conclusion a long time ago that if life isn't fun, you're not doing it right. If helping people with their needs is fun for me, it should, in turn, make their lives more fun.

Fun has to be looked at not as frivolity but rather as enjoyment. Frivolity is superficial to the point of foolishness and is recognized by its lightheartedness and even giddiness. Enjoyment is a state of gratification, pleasure and satisfaction recognized by an inner delight of one's surroundings. Joy is a state of contentment, and contentment is the opposite of need. Joy, then, is not in that which we have gathered about us; it is that which is within us.

RICHARD ROBBINS

# 25

## Chris's Bible

I received two letters from the post office. One of them said, "I know it's early and I know you have a lot to do. Is there anything I can help with?"

I wrote back and thanked her for her offer. I told her that I had just got two new elves and that it looked like everything would be ready by Christmas. "I checked, and you are already on my nice list. Can't wait to see you at Christmas time. Love, Santa."

The second letter was of a more urgent nature. It was from a young girl who seemed to think it was important that we knew she was nine years old. She started her letter:

> I am 9 years old, my name is Suzanne, and I was wondering if you ever gave Christmas presents early. It is not for me. I am 9. It is for my brother Christopher, and he is 7. You won't have to bring him a present at Christmas because he is in the hospital and won't be here for Christmas. He is at the Valley View Hospital in room 323, and he is 7. I'm 9. All he wants is a picture story Bible, one that I can read to him. He can't read yet. I am 9. Mom and Dad helped me write this. They said they could go get him a Bible, but he wants it to come from Santa.

It wasn't whether I could get him a Bible; it was more of how I would get it to him. The hospital was the same one where

Martin was at and the same one I visited last Christmas. Mailing the present from the North Pole seemed somewhat appropriate, but a visit from Santa seemed to be more in order. Do I put on my Santa suit, or do I just dress in a nice suit that wouldn't cause quite as much of a stir in the hospital? I decided to put the question to my elves. Four heads are always better than one.

I called a special meeting because I felt an urgency to fill Christopher's need. Mable and Anne came right over, and with Sarah, we sat as I told them of my dilemma. I could tell much pondering was going on. You could almost hear them thinking.

Ann was the first to voice her thoughts. She said, "Everyone knows that Santa doesn't wear his suit in the middle of summer; it is just too hot."

Sarah added that she didn't like any of the Santa workshop outfits she had seen.

Mable had it all pictured out in her mind: "I see Santa very well dressed in a beautiful, light-colored summer suit, but he has to have one with a vest. We can change the buttons with reindeer or elf buttons. He has to have a red tie with red stockings and a red handkerchief in his pocket. He must wear his Santa glasses and have some sort of a Santa tie pin—maybe even a watch fob and chain on his vest, Santa always had to know the right time."

Mable's idea caught on and even sounded good to me, but where could we get such a suit? We didn't have the time to make it. It was suggested that we go to the Downtown Mall and shop until we could find just the right suit.

Ann suggested that the cost of the suit should be taken out of the Santa fund because it was for Santa purposes.

I got the Jeep ready while they all freshened up, and off we went.

Sarah and I had shopped many times for clothes for me in the past, but three women together was reaching the limits of propriety. I could tell they were having the time of their lives. They hadn't had to shop for a man in some time.

At the third store, which was just a little more expensive than the first two, we found the perfect suit. It was a medium tan in a very good material with a vest. It fit almost perfectly. Only the pants would need tailoring. The store employees said they could have it ready by that same afternoon. Once the suit was chosen, it wasn't hard to pick the right tie, and the one we liked just happened to have a matching handkerchief with it. Santa would surely look presentable and would be able to carry on his identity.

While in the mall we went to a bookstore and in the Christian book section found the perfect illustrated Bible for Christopher. I have always been amazed at how well illustrators were able to follow the stories and make them come alive. I would be proud to present such a compilation.

When we arrived home I penned a letter to Suzanne:

*Suzanne,*

*Thank you for your request for an early Christmas present for your brother. In two days, on Thursday of this week, I plan to visit Christopher in the hospital and present him with the requested Christmas present. I'll get there about two in the afternoon and would like to meet you and your family. If you can't make it, I'll see to it that Christopher gets what he requested.*

*Santa*

I took the letter straight to the post office and paid for next-day delivery to make sure they would be notified.

The next day I went to the men's store to pick up my suit. I found the girl who had helped us. She said, "It's not very often we have a man come in with three women to help him buy a suit. I see you survived the ordeal."

I told her the reason for the visit, and she asked, "Are you the real Santa? Wait a minute, are you *our* Santa?"

I said, "Even Santa needs to get new clothing once in a while."

She was ready to ring up the sale but hesitated and said, "Just a moment; I'll be right back." When she returned, she was all smiles and said, "You get the 40 percent Santa discount." When I told the girls about it, they wondered if there was an elf discount.

There hadn't been time to make the adjustments on the vest buttons or to find a watch chain, but when I got dressed, even I was impressed. With my beard trimmed to perfection, my Santa glasses in place, and a bright red tie, there was a hint that Santa was in the house.

We thought it best that Santa go to the hospital by himself— but only if a full report could be made. The Bible was wrapped in beautiful gold paper. Christopher had to be able to unwrap his gift. There was no doubt about my being recognized as Santa.

As I walked in, Christopher blurted out, "Santa!" It caused me to laugh my Santa laugh, and I was in business.

I said, "You must be Christopher," and he just laughed and said, "And that is Suzanne." She laughed and gave me an uninhibited hug. How can Santa appear happy with tears so near the surface? I shook hands with the parents, and they backed off so the children could have Santa to themselves.

I said, "Christopher, that is a long name. Do they call you Chris?"

"Sometimes," he said.

I told him that I was called *Kris* once in a while—Kris Kringle.

I handed him the package and told him that this was an early Christmas present, and that I hoped it was what he wanted.

He smiled and said, "I know what it is."

He almost reverently opened the package and, at the first glimpse of the Bible, said, "It's just what I wanted."

I had been curious as to why, out of all the gifts he could have asked for, he had desired a Bible. I didn't have to ask the question.

He said, "Do you know why I want a Bible, Santa?"

When I answered that I wasn't sure but that I had some ideas, he said, "I want to know more about God and heaven." And then he added, "You know I am going to go live with Him before too long." It was as though he were looking forward to a trip that was awaiting him. Rather than worry about what was happening to him, he was looking forward to where he was going.

I said my goodbyes to Suzanne and Christopher. She had already started reading and read with a clarity that even I could understand. The gospel seemed to have more meaning coming from a child's mouth.

I went to say goodbye to the parents, and their mother said, "You must have a thousand questions."

I merely stated that I already knew the answers. I only wished I were prepared as well as Christopher to accept the inevitable. If only all the people in the world were so well primed and took the time to get to know God better.

RICHARD ROBBINS

# 26

## *Christmas Preparation*

Christmas was getting closer. My first letters from companies that wanted my Santa services for their parties started to dribble in.

My first letter was from Mrs. Geldenhuys. She informed me that she was no longer the Santa Claus lady and that she had been promoted, which was a result of such a great Christmas party. But she let the girl who took her place know that I was the best-ever Santa and that they wanted to make sure I would be available. I entered the date on the calendar and made a note to follow up with a letter confirming the party.

Martin Burgess, after a full recovery, had returned to work and called to see if I could make a Christmas planning meeting with some of the mall executives. I put my new suit on and noted to myself that I looked for occasions to wear it as I thought I looked quite dapper in it.

I went the very next afternoon to attend the mall's Christmas planning meeting. To my surprise, Kate had been invited. I had wanted to get to know her a little better, so I was happy to see her again.

They had a wonderful rendition of the Santa village with several wonderful additions made to it. Kate was particularly thrilled with what she started calling her stage. It was set almost at the front of the village, and they had depicted an elf standing on it with spotlights shining on her. She would be right out in front where she could be seen by the shoppers as they made their way through the halls. Her songs would be heard over the whole mall through their sound system. Everything seemed to be in order, and I was thrilled at the prospects of coming back for another Christmas.

The mall manager, Haley's father, asked if he could take a few minutes of the meeting. He stood at the head of the conference table and thanked all of us for last year's Christmas successes. He told us that although it had been the most lucrative Christmas season the mall had ever had, it had also been unsurpassed in the Christmas spirit that had been present. He mentioned that our hard work had not gone unnoticed, and he also noticed that we seemed to be enjoying ourselves more. In his own words, he said, "I have come to the conclusion that if we as mall employees do everything we can to help the store owners and the kiosk managers and, more importantly, the public to get into the spirit of Christmas, we will be adding to the joy that should be felt at that time of year."

He continued: "Let's take the business out of Christmas and insert kindness, because kindness is best exhibited by the services we offer. I'm giving you greater leeway in the way you do your jobs this year. Take time to mingle with the crowds and even help in the shops. There are certain standards that must be maintained, but let's all chip in to make our jobs and the store workers' tasks more bearable. Wouldn't it be great if we couldn't wait to come to work each day because we were having so much fun helping others—right down to the mother with a crying baby?"

He then turned to me and said," Santa, we will take your lead. We will merely be asking our employees to follow your example and make this a fun Christmas."

I gave him a smile and a nod and was happy about his approach to this great season, but underneath, I was considering this great responsibility. *I've got to move forward as though the whole success of this year depends on me. Santa can do this. Can I truly be Santa?* I thought. My resolve grew as I determined the obligation I was assuming. Then, as if someone were teaching me a great lesson, the thought sprung into my head: "A job you do because you feel obliged definitely lacks dignity; the best action comes from love, not obligation."

After the meeting and on the way out, Martin caught up with me and let me know that I would be receiving $10,000 for the year, quite a large raise over last year. He also told me that Kate's pay would be higher, considering the fact that she would be an entertainer and not just an all-around helper.

RICHARD ROBBINS

# 27

## *Every Little Helps*

When I arrived home I was informed by Sarah that dinner would not be ready for about an hour. This would give me time to check the mail and e-mail and phone messages, a process that was taking longer each day.

I was surprised to find a phone message from Mr. Harrington. He asked if I would return his call. I called him and he answered. I was always impressed that a man of his stature answered his own phone calls.

When he realized whom he was talking to, his manner changed, and he seemed to be a little excited. "Santa," he said, "I've been meaning to call you for some time. I received a copy of your *Giver Tidings* and was very impressed with how much you accomplished with so little."

I said, "Have you got time for a very little story?"

"From Santa? Yes!" he said

I told him this was a story I had heard long ago and didn't know its source. "There was once a man named Mr. Little, and he was married to Mrs. Little, and they lived in a little house, and had seven little Littles, and got by on very little. The neighbors wondered how Mr. Little and Mrs. Little and the seven little Littles could live in such a little house and get by on so little, so they asked Mr. Little, 'How can you and Mrs. Little and the seven little Littles live in such a little house, and get by on so little?' Mr.

Little answered, 'Every Little helps.' There are a lot of people that can't stand to sit around and just watch others suffer; we had a little help along the way."

I then told Mr. Harrington of the funds I had been receiving from his cohorts, and when he asked if I needed more, I told him that for now we were doing great. "But around Christmas time when the demand is greater, we might have need of more."

He simply said, "Please don't let anyone go without; no degree of sadness should be allowed." He then gave me a sincere thanks and assured me that our city is a better place to live in because we have our own real Santa.

During dinner, the phone rang. It was Mark Peterson, the young man who had called about honoring Mrs. B. He dispensed with any informalities and got right to the problem. He said that he had been working hard on the pledge and after rewriting it many times seemed satisfied with what he had. He had formed a small committee of some of the students who loved Mrs. B as much as he had, but even with all their heads together, they couldn't come up with a proper form to present their pledge to her.

I asked when they were going to present it and was told that at Thanksgiving time, the school had a special assembly put on by the students annually. They had convinced the principal to let them use the whole assembly to present a *This Is Your Life, Mrs. B.* type of program." There was still plenty of time before Thanksgiving to prepare, but they didn't want to leave it until the last minute. They would have a lot of signatures to collect.

I told him to e-mail what they had over to me and I would put one of my elves on the job.

He promised that he would have it to me tonight and then said, "Feel free to make any changes you think may enhance the pledge."

I could hardly wait to see what they had come up with.

When I did finally receive Mark's e-mail with the pledge attached, I went to my office where I could read it and give it the time and thought it might need. I told Sarah that I might be up a little later and told her to go to bed when she felt like it. I opened the document on my computer and began what I thought would be an evaluation most possibly with recommendations for changes. What I read instead was a heartfelt offering that only a person who had intimate knowledge of another could offer.

From school records, each student's name would be added and a signature would be signed as the students were found. This pledge would hang in the school award case for one year for past students to come by and sign it, and then it would be delivered to Mrs. B. It was a beautiful sentiment.

In the morning when I called Barbara, I told her of the project and read her the pledge.

She was completely on board. She said, "It sounds like a beautiful scroll would be in order. I'll get right to work on it. I see a dowel roller with elaborate gold ends and one long sheet of rolled papyrus-like paper. When rolled up, it can be tied with a small golden braid with tassels on each end to match the roller ends."

It sounded wonderful to me and would certainly be fitting of a ceremonial function. I e-mailed the document over to her, and the process began.

I called Mark back and told him I hadn't changed one word, and thought the sentiment to be beautiful. I also told him that I had the document being constructed, and that I would need the names and the class years of all of Mrs. B's students as soon as I could get them.

He said there was a gap of two years in the school records, but they believed they could reconstruct them and would have them to me as soon as possible.

# 28

## *Empathy*

The experience with Mark led me to ponder about how important empathy is in the life of a person. Every human being has a deep feeling for their needs to at least be recognized. When they realize that we recognize their need and it hurts us as much as it hurts them, it is the beginning of healing. I learned from study that empathy comes from the Greek word pathos, which is also the Greek word for healing.

It appears that problems we experience in life give us a degree of knowledge as to how others feel when they are going through similar difficulties. We actually know how they feel. You can feel sorry for a person and feel sympathy, but unless you have felt the actual pain, you may not be able to feel empathy. The feeling of empathy takes place only when you really care. But does this mean you have to know the person?

Recently when I was sitting on a bench in the mall observing people, I noticed a young mother coming toward me with her daughter. Her daughter was walking barefooted. Ignoring me, they sat on the bench next to me, and the mother said, "You must wear your shoes in the mall."

The little girl answered, "I don't want to, they hurt my feet."

Thinking I might be able to talk the girl into wearing her shoes, Super Santa stepped in. I turned to the girl and said, "I don't like wearing shoes either. Do you think it would look funny if you saw me walking through the mall barefooted?"

She gave a little laugh, and I said, "Where are your shoes? Maybe we can stretch them just a little to make them more comfortable."

She reached into her mother's purse and pulled out a much-worn pair of shoes.

I could tell that they had been stretched about as far as they could be. I said after fussing around with one of them, "There let's try this one on."

It was evident it was much too small. The mother looked at me in an apologetic manner and said, "Our budget just won't allow for a pair of shoes right now."

I took her by the hand and said, "I know just how you're feeling. I have, in times past, been unable to provide my children with their basic needs, and it's not a good feeling is it? I also know how your daughter feels because when I was young, I had to wear a pair of shoes that was way too small and hurt my feet."

We agreed, and that agreement made us one. When I asked if I might be able to purchase her daughter some new shoes, she didn't hesitate to say yes. She instinctively knew that she would be relieving my sorrow as much as her own. She could tell that I felt bad for them and that I cared.

We went to a children's shoe store and purchased two pairs of shoes—one to play in and one to dress in. I felt so comforted and relieved. I actually felt that they had empathy for me in letting me do this deed, and I put my emotions to rest.

I wondered if people have to experience every sorrow in life before they can be empathetic to similar sorrows. I came to the conclusion that you don't have to have been blind to feel what a blind man feels, and you don't have to be palsied to realize the restrictions it submits you to. The most empathetic man to ever live felt their sorrow and healed them and, to those who had done wrong, forgave them.

It seemed important for Santa to gain the ability to feel and share another person's emotions. Santa has to be caring, so I asked myself, *Can empathy be developed? And if so, how?*

Through experience, I felt that my degree of empathy increased almost daily, but how was that happening? I came to the conclusion that I was taking more time to consider the feelings of others, but more importantly, I was taking the time to find out my own feelings. When you consider how you feel about how they feel, it gives a better reference as to how others feel when faced with life's problems. When I can sense the emotions of another person, I can understand and communicate with them and their perspective on life.

There is a side benefit to empathy. When you enter into another person's feeling, sometimes those emotions are happiness and joy. Elation and empathy allow you to match those feelings, and your life is enhanced by those moments.

As Santa, I pretty well followed the old saying: "If I could dry your tears, I would. If I could take the pain, I would. But all I have are eyes to cry with you, arms for you to run to, and a promise that you'll never bear the pain alone, because I'm here."

RICHARD ROBBINS

# 29

## Mable's Project

I was soon learning that *being* Santa is much harder than *becoming* Santa.

To be Santa, I had to exist in actuality; I had to equal him in identity. I was also learning that the rewards were worth any effort needed to reach that ultimate goal. The real truth of the matter was that I was wondering if I would ever be satisfied. It seemed that when I reached one level, I learned that there was much more I needed to accomplish. The small list I had started with—love, giving, understanding, appreciation, and empathy— just seemed to grow.

I remembered where I was not even a year ago and felt somewhat satisfied with what I had achieved. I was certainly enjoying life more. This just led me to believe that the sooner I could gain all the characteristics of Santa, the more I would enjoy life.

You can always make changes to your character. The important thing is to know what character you want to be. Santa's reputation was impeccable; I believed it was because of decisions he has made. Proper decisions can be made only when facts are understood and priorities are in order. Priorities should place decisions in the order of their importance and the urgency of the need.

Another month had passed, and time seemed to be flying. I wasn't worried because we had been preparing well for Christmas.

It was Thursday and time for another nightly meeting.

Barbara had not attended all of our meetings because of family implications, but she was here tonight. She had brought with her the drawings for the scrolls to be presented to Mrs. B.

We began our meeting with prayer, something we had decided to do from the beginning. We just thought we could use all the help we could get. Our meetings were all business. Ann read the minutes, we had follow-up reports, and the new Santa suit would be finished as soon as the buttons arrived from Switzerland. We had agreed to order these buttons because they were less expensive. Of course with the added shipping expense they were about the same price, but they were of a much superior quality and would be unique in our area. The elf costume was completed. Kate would be able to come when invited for a fitting, and we determined that this could wait until the Santa suit was also completed.

I also brought them up to date on a couple of Santa expenditures that involved helping a widow with her heating bill payment, and providing a young man with a pair of little-league baseball shoes and a special bat we decided to throw in.

We then got down to new business, and Barbara showed us her sketches of the pledge scrolls. Whenever she opened her large presentation envelopes, it made you feel as if you were looking at a great piece of art for the first time. The design was feminine in every way. It even had a carrying case designed that the scroll would fit into. We had found out Mrs. B's first name was Mary Lou, and it was handwritten in a beautiful gold lettering on the outside of the case: *Mrs. Mary Lou Burningham.*

We enthusiastically gave our approval, and let Barbara know that funds were available, and reminded her that she should let us know the cost.

In the other business category, which we sometimes placed under the needs agenda, Mable presented to us a circumstance she had run across. She and one of her daughters went into a restaurant to have dinner. A very polite and seemingly well-educated young man waited on them. "Well, you know me. Before long, I had his whole life story!" she said.

He had graduated over a year ago at our local college, and he still hadn't found satisfactory employment. His wife was working as a secretary, and he baby sat their daughter during the day while she worked, and then he waited tables at night. Mable had pictured in her mind a couple who never got to spend any time together. I said, "It is a scenario that happens all too often."

We decided that I should go to the restaurant, find the young man, and set up an appointment to find out how we could help him. Like a true investigator, Mable already had his name and his work schedule. It so happened that he worked the next evening.

I went to the restaurant to meet him. I asked the girl at the cash register if Allen Birch was working, and she said she would find him for me.

He was a very nice-looking young man with a very agreeable personality. We sat at a booth, and I told him about the woman he had waited on who had found out all about his job situation.

He laughed a little and said, "Oh! You must mean Mable. She is not a lady one would easily forget. She found out so much about me that I thought she might be writing a book."

I said, "You have the right lady. Anyway, I thought we might be of help to you in finding you a proper placement in a good company."

He of course asked if I represented an employment agency.

I let him know that I had once hired and placed many people in jobs, but that I was now retired and just thought he might need some help. He had a hard time believing that someone would take the time to do such a thing. When I asked him if he had a resume and if he would be willing to send it over to me, he was more than willing.

When I asked him to write me a one-page explanation of what type of work he really wanted to do and what his qualifications were to accomplish this work, he told me he might have to take a day to write this out. I gave him my e-mail address, which surprised him a little.

He asked, "What do you have to do with Santa?"

"Everything," I answered.

Two days passed before I received Allen Birch's information. His resumé was complete, and I could see that no adjustments were needed. He had graduated with a master's in business administration, and his bachelor's degree was in computer science. He had graduated with honors. This young man was no slouch, and, in fact, he may have been overqualified for our job market. His letter said that he loved to be involved in the design of computer programs. His background in business would allow him to complete necessary market research to determine programs that may be needed.

I was impressed, and would start the ball rolling. From my own contacts with companies I had done business with, I would make calls to the personnel directors I knew personally. I thought this might be a chance for Mr. Harrington to get involved physically and not just monetarily. Allen had accomplished what the world had told him he needed to do to achieve, and now the world needed to step up and reward him for his diligence.

My first call was to Mr. Harrington. He had a lot of contacts, and while I was working on mine, he could be working on his. He answered the phone again. I said, "Hello, this is Santa."

He replied, "That's not a call you get very often! What can I do for you?"

I said, "I have a situation here that, if not taken care of, will lead to a family not having a very good Christmas." I went into the details of Allen Birch's story, and Mr. Harrington seemed to be very sympathetic.

"I think that is a situation we have all found ourselves in at one time—coming right out of college and not having a job to go to," he said. "Santa, is this something you would allow me to handle? Give me a few days, and I'll get back to you."

I told him I would e-mail him all the information and thanked him for his assistance. I chose to wait on making further calls because I didn't think the problem could be in any better hands.

I just didn't know if I could sit on the sidelines and wait for the results. A young family's future was at stake, and feeling that you might be a part of making that a good future was very satisfying. When you can't do anything about what is happening, you sometimes become anxious. Nervousness, even apprehension and fretfulness, sets in, but you must stay enthusiastic and eager and must wait for good things to happen.

I called Mable and brought her up to date. I told her that I had the largest businessman in the area finding Allen a job.

Her reaction said it all for me: "We can make a difference, can't we?"

I thought to myself, *This is what we do. We change people. We just have to make certain that we change them for the better.*

True to his word, two days later, I received a call from Mr. Harrington. He said, "I hope you don't mind, but I called Allen Birch myself and have set up an appointment to interview him tomorrow afternoon at 1 p.m. I would love it if you could be there for the interview. I think we have found a place for him in the marketing department of our corporate offices. His job would be to evaluate our holding companies' marketing programs and make suggestions for improvement. He was very excited when I discussed it with him. This is an area that needs attention in our business, and quite frankly I think he would be perfect for the position.

I let Mr. Harrington know that I would be there and thanked him for the opportunity.

And then he said, "If you're like me, you like to see something through to the finish."

The next day at 1 p.m., I found myself sitting in the lobby outside of Mr. Harrington's office. It wasn't too long before Allen joined me. He looked at me and shook his head and asked if I was responsible for this meeting. "No. Mable was," I told him.

Mr. Harrington's assistant walked over to us and told us we could go in now. When we walked in, Mr. Harrington grabbed my hand and said, "Hello Santa. Welcome!"

Allen looked at me and just began laughing. He said, "Is this really happening?" Mr. Harrington was taken in by his naiveté and openness, and a rapport was begun on the spot.

I think both Allen and Mr. Harrington were better off for their relationship, and I felt good that we were a part of it. On the way out, I asked Allen who had the baby while he was being interviewed, and was told that Mable had called and had volunteered to baby-sit. I later found that Mable was ecstatic because the baby would now have a mother home with it every day.

Allen asked if he could start in two weeks, which would give his wife time to give notice to her work. At our next meeting, we made a note to drop them off a special present at Christmas time, just so they could remember the time Santa helped out.

# 30

## *New Elf, New Costume*

It was fitting time for the Santa and elf costumes. We decided to make a party out of it. I called Kate's house, and her mother answered. I introduced myself and told her that a week from Thursday we were going to have a party at our home. I said that Kate's elf costume had been completed and that we were going to try on my new Santa suit and her elf costume.

She said, "Let me get Kate, she'll be so excited."

Kate came on the line and asked "Is this Santa?"

When I answered yes, she said, "It's going to take me some time to get used to receiving calls from Santa Claus."

I told her about the party and invited her to bring her parents. I said, "Your elf costume is completed, and we want to make sure it will fit."

As if reading my mind, she said, "Can I sing you one of my Christmas song arrangements? I just want to make sure that it will be okay."

I told her she could sing as many as she wanted. "We have a piano, and my wife can play for you, I added."

"Oh, I hope you don't mind, but I like to play for myself," she said.

The very next morning I called Martin Burgess and asked him how hard it would be to have a piano on Kate's stage because she likes to accompany herself.

He said, "We have a piano company in the mall; and I'll bet if we let them put an advertising sign on the piano, they will provide it free."

I thought to myself, *She could also accompany group singing.* This seemed to sparkle my imagination.

Thursday night everyone came early. Barbara placed her package on the coffee table, which already had two large, well-wrapped packages on it. Introductions were made, and each of us told a little bit about ourselves. I was surprised when I learned that Ann had been the seamstress for our local opera company for almost ten years of her life. Mable, not to be outdone, told us she had written a gossip column for our local newspaper in her younger life. There were a few snickers, but Mable's glare put a stop to any comments.

Barbara added that she was now the art director for a large advertising company, and it was her dream that someday she could just spend her time painting anything she wanted to.

Kate took her turn in stride and said, "I'm just a student," and sat down.

I stood up and said, "I am just Santa Claus," and sat down.

There was some hand clapping, and I went on to say, "Kate has agreed to play and sing a Christmas song for us just to get us in the mood before we open the packages."

Kate went to the piano with no music and began playing "Santa Claus Is Coming to Town." She sang to us as if we were a group of children and started out with a very slow, drawn-out tempo that was designed to make sure we were listening. It just got faster as she sang: *"You'........d be......tter wa........ tch ou.......t, You'.....d be......tter no.....t cr.....y, You'...d be...tter no...t pou...t, I...m tell...ing yo.u wh.y, Santa Claus is coming to town."*

Her plea for us to be nice was heartfelt, and Santa Claus's coming to town was the event of the year. You could never tire of hearing her smooth, warm expressive voice. She put meaning into each word, and the message of the song was delivered in a way that you understood its meaning. The good thing about it was that I would get to hear her sing for a whole month. Everyone there utterly enjoyed the song and wanted to hear more.

We opened Barbara's scroll offering first. It was exactly as she had told me earlier. In a beautiful, matching presentation box was the scroll. It had a dowel at the top and at the bottom to roll the document on, and at the ends of each dowel were ornamental gold caps. The scroll had a gold-braid rope tied around them with gold tassels at the ends. Mark's exact words were penned in a beautiful calligraphy script that indicated to those presenting the pledge cared enough to have it hand made.

The scroll was long enough for all the signatures from all the students she had ever taught. All the students' names, the year they took her class, and a space for their signature were included. Blank spaces were left in case they had missed any students.

Barbara had told me that she and Mark had become good friends on the phone and that they thought the list to be complete. It would be impossible to collect every signature, but Mrs. B would have the names of every student she had ever taught.

Also in the box was a large holder for the scroll. It would keep it protected, and it was done in a much heavier material and had an envelope flap to open for insertion. This large envelope also had a gold ribbon tied around it. All of the paper was matching and was done in a deep ivory color. We told everyone the story behind the scroll and introduced them to the idea that we do a lot more than just hand out candy canes at the mall.

Kate opened her package next. The elf costume was almost a duplicate of Haley's from last year. The only addition is what Ann called a music case. It was constructed of the same material as her dress but would allow her to keep her music ready. We found out later that the case wasn't needed because Kate played all of her music by ear, a talent very few possess.

Kate stood and looked into her box and said, "Is this really happening to me? I don't know what to say, this is all so awesome!" Tears started to form, and Sarah and Mable both offered tissues and hugs. Once again, a little family had formed and love was immediate.

Ann and Mable both arose to present me with my new Santa suit. They did it in a very over-exaggerated way, as though they were introducing the latest fashions.

Mable said, "This year Santa will be featured in a rich crimson red, thick pile-plush jacket with satin lining and long-hair faux fur trim with matching satin-lined pants."

Ann continued, "The same thick pile-plush hat with satin lining and matching fur trim will complete the ensemble."

They went on to say, "And this year Santa will have his own black leather strap with jingle bells on it to start each occasion off with the joy of the season."

After the laughter was over, Kate and I retired to our dressing rooms to make sure everything fit perfectly. I came out first and the suit brought the expected approval.

Kate didn't come out for a while. Sarah went in to check on her. She was putting on each item very slowly while admiring how each addition enhanced her looks. We learned much later that Kate had not been used to getting a lot of new clothing, and she was taking the time to discover this new feeling.

She walked out as though reborn and went right to the piano. As she sat down, she said, "Excuse me, I just have to do this." She then played a beautiful rendition of "Joy to the World." It wasn't hard, seeing her dedication to this song, to understand her true nature—she loved the purpose of Christmas.

Sarah and I were tidying up after everyone had left, and I could tell she had something on her mind. She was making what I called her thoughtful moves, very deliberate and much slower than she usually moved. It was as though she didn't want her contemplations interrupted even by her movement.

I learned long ago if I disturbed her by asking, "What are you thinking about," she would just say, "Oh nothing." But if I let her complete her thought processes, it was usually worth the patience.

She finally said, "Did you notice how quiet Kate's parents were tonight? They hardly said two words."

I had noticed it but hadn't given it much thought.

She added, "They seemed to enjoy themselves, and on the way out, her mother said, "Thanks for giving Kate this opportunity." But other than that, it's about all I heard.

I said, "Well we certainly don't have enough information to draw any conclusions, so let's wait and see what develops."

The problem with Sarah's thinking is that it always starts me to thinking. I was sure that I would get to know Kate's parents better as the year went along, especially if I made excuses to visit them.

RICHARD ROBBINS

# 31

## A New Dad for Christmas

It is sometimes hard to understand people, but all people can be understood. I believe that if we don't understand why people are the way they are, it is because of a lack of effort on our part. There must be a reason why people act as they do. If we gain a little information or knowledge about them and use our senses to proceed to understand them, then we will find their reasons. It is not until you understand or perceive and comprehend the nature of the person that you can help them. Knowledge is the beginning of wisdom.

One of the last children's letters I had received just after last Christmas was from a young boy that said,

*Dear Santa,*
*Can you please get me a younger dad for Christmas?*

*Jamie Withers.*

Because Christmas was over, I was very busy at the time and I placed the letter in a follow-up folder and put it in my files. I don't like anything sitting in my follow-up files for long, so I pulled it out and wrote him a letter back and said:

*I'm sorry I didn't get your letter until Christmas was over. I'll see about getting you a new dad by next Christmas.*

*P.S. How old do you want your new father to be?*

*Santa.*

It wasn't too long before I received another letter, this time from Kyle Withers. It read:

*Dear Santa,*

*I was opening the mail this evening and saw a letter addressed to my son from you. Needless to say, I was quite disturbed by its content. Could you please write back and let me know why you will be giving my son a new father for next Christmas?*

*Kyle Withers*

And I wrote back:

*Dear Mr. Withers,*

*Your son wrote me and asked if he could have a younger father. He is on my nice list, so I thought I would see what I could do. Did you pass my letter on to your son? I wouldn't want him to think that Santa is ignoring him.*

*P.S. Why would your son want a younger father? How old are you?*

*Santa*

I was sure that this was a case of the father not understanding a son's needs and vice versa. Sometimes understanding can come easily if a problem is just brought to light.

The next letter I received was from Jamie. He said:

*I don't know how old I want him to be, but can you make sure he can throw a ball and go fishing?*
*Jamie Withers*

The next letter I received was from the father, who said:

*I read my son's last letter to you before he sent it. I think I have an understanding of why my son wants a new father. Before you send him one, will you please give me time to have a discussion with him? By the way, I am only 32 years old and do know how to throw a ball and fish.*

I penned this note back:

*Dear Mr. Withers,*
*I figured that you may be able to work this out. I'm glad that you are able to because it is not really easy to find new fathers, and once found, they usually don't always seem to fit the bill as well as the old ones. Let me know if I can help.*
*Santa*

I thought our letter writing might be over, but a few days later, one last letter came from Jamie. It said:

*Dear Santa,*
*Instead of getting me a new dad for Christmas, could I have some baseballs and a couple of fishing poles?*
*Jamie*

This one couldn't wait. I drove to the nearest sporting goods store where I picked up a box of baseballs, two fishing reels and poles, and a tube for the poles. After stopping at home for Sarah to get them postal ready and long enough for me to write another letter, I took them to the post office and mailed them. The letter said:

Dear Jamie and Father,
    Here are the Christmas presents you requested. I'm sending them long before Christmas while the weather is still somewhat good and you can use them now. And Jamie, I'm glad you kept your dad.

    Santa

# 32

## Company Party Agenda

It seemed like the longer I was Santa, the easier it was to be Santa. It wasn't that the nature of the work got any easier, but that my abilities were improving.

I had sent out a mailing to all of the companies where I had been Santa last year. Even though it was only the end of August, I had received affirmative replies from all but two of them. Their requests were almost duplicated: could we have you longer for the party? ...We're willing to pay more. Some already knew their dates and I filled them in on the calendar. I could see that there would have to be some adjustments made.

I had an idea and thought I would try it out on Mrs. Geldenhuys. But before I called her, I called Kate.

Kate had her own cell phone, which made it very convenient for me. When she answered, I asked her if she would like to make just a little more money for Christmas.

She said, "You know I'd do it for free, don't you? But a little money would sure help with my college tuition."

I told her about the company Christmas parties and said, "I think they would be delighted to have a singing elf and also someone who could accompany them while they sang Christmas carols."

She thought it would be great but needed her parents' approval.

I said, "Let me know as soon as possible."

She said she would call them right now and get right back to me.

I did get a callback, but it was her father, who said, "I hope you don't mind but Kate is our only child, and we might be a little overprotective of her. Are these parties she's talking about of a wild nature—are people drinking at them?"

I answered that some do and some don't, and then I told him that I never attended a party last year that got out of hand or wasn't uplifting in nature. I told him that I intended to drive both of us to the party and afterward to deliver her safely home. I wouldn't ask without taking full responsibility for her. I still sensed a hesitation, so I told him to think about it and to take the time he needed to make a good decision.

He said, "Thank you, I won't leave you hanging."

I felt good about Kate's father's concern. I certainly wouldn't be upset if she was not allowed to come with me to the parties. I wish I would have given a little more contemplation to a lot of the decisions I had made about my own kids while they were growing up. I've never doubted a mother's intuition about her children, but never did I think of a father as capable of having instincts that would warn him of the dangers of the world.

When Kate called me later and said she could do it, I said, "I guess your father has a lot of faith in you."

She said something simple then, something that I will never forget, and it gave me an appreciation for her parents. She stated, "He just had to have some time to pray about it."

As we were getting ready for bed that night, I told Sarah about my idea for Kate and how her father had given his approval and then said, "Remember how quiet her parents were at the party? You said you thought they enjoyed themselves. I think I've figured it out. People express their joy in many different ways. I think people who have a spiritual nature tend to understand life on a higher level and may express themselves more inwardly than outwardly. I just remember from reading the scriptures that the Savior felt the joy within His heart. Many times, it says, that his soul delighted, but I can never remember it saying that he felt so great that he laughed out loud."

I continued, "When I picture Him being happy, I picture a beautiful smile on his face, a nod of his head, and even a hug. Santa could follow no greater example."

Sarah turned over, gave me a good night kiss, and said, "I've known that all along."

I called Mrs. Geldenhuys the next day. When she answered, I said, "What's this about not being the Santa Claus lady anymore?"

She replied, "I got promoted."

I told her that I thought being the Santa Claus lady was the highest job in any company.

She said, "This doesn't take me off your nice list, does it?"

After a moment of thought, I said, "Not if you tell me who took over your position."

"You've already met her," she said. "She was my assistant and brought you to my office the first time you came. She's already been filled in, by me, about Christmas. Are you going to be able to make our program longer for us?"

After a brief chat and an assurance that I would be with them again and that I would stay longer, she said, "Let me transfer you over to Gloria."

Gloria answered immediately.

"Ms. Haws?" I said, "we'll have to do something about that 'Ms.' I already know what to get you for Christmas."

She blurted out, "Is this Santa? They warned me about you."

We both had a good laugh. I could remember her as a very kind person who was also very efficient. I said, "I understand that you are the lady now in charge of Santa and was told you want a longer party this year. I have a suggestion to make that I hope you'll like. I have an elf working with me at the mall this year. She is a senior in high school and is 18 years old. This girl plays the piano and can play any Christmas song upon request and sings like a lark. I'd like to suggest that I bring her along with me. She could sing a couple of songs and then accompany a sing along on the piano. The increased amount you mean to pay me for staying longer could be given to her; my pay would remain the same. Let's say the whole program would only cost $150."

Gloria was delighted and told me that it was a done deal. Kate should be thrilled with $50 for a little over an hour's work.

I wanted to get the news to Kate and called her right away. She was very excited to hear the news, and when I told her she would be getting $50 for each party, she could hardly believe it.

She said, "How many of these parties are there?"

I told her I did 48 last year but didn't know if every company would agree to our proposal.

She did the quick math and said, "That would be $2,400 in one month. Wow!" The phone went silent. I waited as she came back on and she commented, "I'm so glad I volunteered as a candy striper. None of this would have happened if I hadn't met you at the hospital."

I've heard the saying "One good deed deserves another," but here it was in action. I asked myself out loud, "Can you ever go wrong by doing good?"

When a good deed is completed, a person will always receive a benefit for doing it. The settlement is not always obvious and hardly ever immediate and usually never monetary in nature. Those doing the deed might recognize the compensation some-where along the way and realize why they are being so fortunate. If receivers are not aware of the recompense, it may be because they haven't taken time to evaluate a change in their lives. This is why it is important to count your blessings on a daily basis. Kate's recognition of her blessings was a credit to her.

I had a lot of phone calls to make and a lot of convincing to do. To my amazement, almost all of the companies looked forward to having more Christmas entertainment. Kate and I would have to sit down and discuss the perfect company Christmas party. I looked at it as a fun assignment. Maybe we could get our other elves to throw in suggestions.

# 33

## *Being Kind to Others*

The next day, Sarah and I were on a grocery expedition stocking up for the coming weeks. It was Sarah who drew my attention to a young couple whose shopping habits were a little difficult to understand. As they went from aisle to aisle, the young man would keep putting items in their cart, and the young woman would take them out and set them back on the shelf. It wasn't as if the items were nonessentials. Most of them seemed to be what was necessary to run a household, and he wasn't trying to load up on goodies.

It wasn't until we were on the same aisle and looking for the same item that we caught a bit of their conversation. We overheard the wife saying, "I know we need that, and it would be nice to have, but we just don't have the money."

We went around the end of the aisle, and Sarah said, "Isn't there something we can do for them, Robert?"

My first thought was to go the checkout counter and tell them to check the young couple out but tell them the items had been paid for. The problem with this is that they wouldn't have many of the items they really should have. A plan came to mind, and I said, "Come on Sarah, follow my lead."

We came around the corner and were face to face with the young couple. I said hello to them and got a nice hello back. I asked in an open way, "You're newlyweds, aren't you?"

I got a positive answer and found out that they had just got off their honeymoon, which had been a nice two-day trip for them. They were on their first shopping trip together.

I turned to Sarah and said, "Do you remember our first shopping trip honey?"

She picked right up on it and said, "It wasn't much fun."

I said, "We couldn't even afford a bottle of dish washing soap by the time we bought a few of the other necessities. We didn't have a lot left to buy food.

Sarah couldn't wait any longer and said, "Would you allow us to help you out a little so you can get started off on the right foot?"

The young man was halfway through his sentence and said, "We couldn't ask you—."

His wife cut him off and said to us, "I think it would be appropriate," and to her husband, "I don't think they would offer if it would be hard on them, and someday we'll repay them by doing the same to someone else.

"Yes," she told us, "we'll do it on one condition, and that is if you will come over and let us cook you a nice dinner some night."

Her husband added that she was a really good cook.

I had decided much earlier that I would always carry a substantial amount of cash for just such an occasion, and I handed them $500. This was much more than they expected and assured us that it would be used to stock their cupboards.

After an exchange of addresses and phone numbers, as we were leaving I overheard the husband say, "Let's start over."

I recorded all of these events, even the details of the experience, with Kate. The *Givers Tidings* would bring the news to those who gave and would allow them the same joys we were experiencing. Who knows—they might see a young couple in a store and do likewise. The more that good could be observed, the more likely good would be done, which would always result in making a better world.

I have always believed that if you're kind to individuals, they will, in turn, be kind to others. This thought had no sooner come to my mind when something happened that proved it. As I was pulling out of the parking lot of the grocery store, another car was pulling out at the same time. I stopped and waved him on. He waved a thank-you back and drove off. He had not gone a couple of yards when another car started pulling out by him, so he stopped this time and gave the others the go-ahead.

Kindness is contagious, and it reflects the best of feelings. The whole concept of kindness is to never have contact with a person who doesn't leave your presence without feeling better. I firmly believe that the reason I love being Santa so much is that I go out each day with the intent to find someone to be kind to. You can never be kind to persons that somehow in their mind don't think of how nice you were, and they are then in turn nicer to others. I believed that when I could even be kind to unkind people, I will have reached my goal. They are the ones who need kindness the most.

My next-door neighbor leaned toward unkindness. It was even hard to get him to say good morning when we met watering a lawn or taking out the garbage. This has been going on for years. I have always pictured myself living in a neighborhood where people were friendly toward one another. Relationships were important to me. Here I was, Santa, and I couldn't even solve a problem next door to me.

In my discussing it with Sarah one night, she said, "What have you done so far to help him be friendly?"

I answered her, "Not much, it's not that he is unkind; it's just that he is not kind."

Sarah merely said, "If you do nothing, I doubt that he will ever change. I don't think he's too friendly, but I feel safe around him."

Late that afternoon I was reading an article our church had sent around, and it spoke of loving our neighbors. It once again returned my thoughts to Jeff Holmes, my next-door neighbor. Something Sarah had said got me thinking. She had said that she felt safe around him. I heard him out mowing his lawn and thought this might be a good time to approach him with a problem I was having.

I walked out the front door and could tell he was surprised when I walked right up to him. Characteristically, he didn't say a word, though he did stop his lawn mower. I asked him if he had a minute, and he gave a positive nod.

I said, "Jeff, I have a problem and was hoping you could help me out with it. Please don't feel obligated if it is not something you could or want to do. I don't know if you have noticed, but I have taken on the job of being Santa Claus. My work takes me to the local mall on weekdays and company parties at night. This makes it so that I am very rarely home the last week of November and the month of December. I just need someone close to keep an eye out if my wife may need some help. She said last week that she felt safe having you as a neighbor. I wouldn't want you to change your lifestyle or anything, just keep an ear open."

His answer surprised me and left me a little humbled. He said, "I saw you in that Santa suit get up last year and thought you made a pretty good Santa. When I noticed how much you were gone, I kept my eye on your place. Won't be any trouble to continue doing it."

I realized that although I had all of the social refinements of being a person who was outgoing and friendly, I had tendencies to be unkind at times. My appraisal of my neighbor, who I found not to be deficient in humane and kindly feelings, diminished my capacity to love him because I had considered him to be unkind. I would have many, probably short, conversations with him in the future. I thought to myself, *I wonder if all this time he has thought me to be unfriendly, and even unkind to him.*

# 34

## *The Candy Shop*

The next morning I went into the bathroom and looked into our wall-size mirror and said, "Good morning, Santa!"

The reflection certainly portrayed a Santa image. It was true that each morning upon awakening, I experienced again a supreme pleasure—that of being Santa Claus. But I also realized that being Santa was no ordinary job. I wanted to *be* Santa; I wanted that to be my identity. I wanted to be Santa when I was just being myself. I wanted others to know that when I'm around them, I am Santa. If I have to tell others that I am Santa, I'm not. It's when a person leans down to a child and whispers, "He's Santa," —that's when you know you're the *real* Santa.

I've asked myself the question, and I'm sure others have wondered also: *Why do I so want to be Santa Claus?* The most truthful answer I have come up with for myself is: *To me, having kids is the ultimate blessing in the world, and that is why I want to be Santa. Everyone in the world is your kid; and once again, the kid's age does not matter.* So I would just keep on doing and learning; it was well worth the effort.

It was Thursday night. I had invited Kate and her parents over to our meeting because we would be discussing the mall presentation and programs for all the company parties.

Kate arrived first but without her parents. She told me that her dad had total trust in her, and that she should learn how to get along by herself.

It wasn't long before the whole team arrived. We said a beginning prayer. Heaven knows that we can use all the help we can get. And then Ann went through the agenda with us.

When we got to items under weekly reporting, I told them about the young couple whom Sarah and I met in the grocery store. They thought we had made a good decision, and Ann deducted $500 from our financial report. There were several other small items we also deducted.

When we got to the discussion phase of the agenda, I asked if we could talk about the procedure for mall strategy. I especially wanted their input, even Kate's, in case I was missing any opportunities. I said, "I'll tell you how it worked out last year, and you tell me if we could improve it."

I told them that the Santa Village at the mall was a very informal setting. Neither Haley, my elf last year, nor I sat down very much. We wandered freely among the crowds that had come to see Santa, and posed for pictures, which they took themselves. Haley felt free to grab her flute and play a Christmas song anytime she felt like it—the more often the better.

I told them all that this year we would have a special stage with a piano on it for Kate, and she could play the piano, or play and sing at any time. She would have a microphone that allowed her songs to be heard through the whole mall.

At this, Kate was getting more excited by the minute. Kate said, "I loved the way last year's elf would just wander among the children playing her flute. It was almost magical. If I had a few songs, backup music could be prerecorded, so I could just take the microphone with me and sing to the children—and maybe even have them sing with me—even form little groups or duets with them. I think it would add a lot, and who knows, Santa, maybe we could even sing a song or two together."

Her enthusiasm was contagious. I think we all wanted to start singing right then.

You could tell Mable couldn't wait to add her input. She said, "I have an idea for the giveaway candy. When I was a little girl, we used to go to the penny candy store, and it was one of the highlights of my youth. I think we should have a candy store where they could choose the kind of candy they want. Tucked away in a corner of Santa's Village, we could have a candy display with all sizes of jars holding their own special candy. There could be one bowl for little foil-wrapped chocolate Santa Clauses; a smaller, round, cuplike dish to hold candy cane sticks; a fish bowl to hold Christmas-designed whipped taffy; Santa lollipops; jars of Tootsie rolls, peppermint twists, and red and green M&M's. I think you get the idea. There are hundreds of Christmas candy offerings, and it all could be so cute. It could become a mall tradition: 'Come and visit Santa's Candy Shop.'"

Well, everyone thought it a marvelous idea, including me. Now all I would have to do is sell it to the mall management.

Barbara volunteered to draw up a layout for such a display. She said that she could remember last year's layout and already had several ideas.

Turning our attention to company parties, I told them I could really use some help with new ideas. For the lack of a better title, we talked about Santa and Christmas jokes, witticisms, anecdotes, tales, or just plain ole stories. "Could I give you all a homework assignment to help me with this by our next meeting? And, could you give suggestions as to who will receive the token of appreciation in our city this year?

We drew the meeting to a close and, as usual, Sarah had a nice refreshment for us. The general conversation while eating our dessert went in the direction of, "There is a lot more to being Santa than meets the eye—especially if you're going to be the real Santa." I loved it that my elves were taking this opportunity seriously.

I was very careful, however, not to make what they were doing seem like work. If they were not having fun, then we were not completing our purpose. I had to remind myself of that several times—not that being Santa had started to be a drudgery, but that being Santa was so much fun that I always wondered if I were working hard enough.

If something is fun, it is pleasant, enjoyable, and usually not serious. A lot of us feel that if you deviate from being serious about life, you don't know what life is all about. Life should be taken seriously, and we should look at the outcome of all of our actions. I believe that is why life should be fun.

This doesn't mean we should be joking or clowning around or being nonsensical. You must never let horseplay or mocking or playing around be a substitute for real enjoyment.

It was during this line of thinking when I came across a great truth. I was finding that when you think of fun as *joy*, you put life in its proper perspective. A statement came to mind that has helped me throughout my life: *If having fun is all there is to life, then the monkey has the man outdistanced—both in amusing and in being amused.*

# 35

## Our Christmas Baby

My church has always taught that, "Man is that he might have joy, and that he might have life more abundantly." I have a block of wood on my desk that has written on it a quote from Marianne Williamson. It reads, "Joy is what happens when we allow ourselves to recognize how good things really are."

If our ultimate goal in life is to have joy, it would be important for Santa to have a good understanding of joy. I found several definitions for joy, and it was easy to find out what it is. But I never thought a person could truly know what joy is until experiencing it.

The best way I could describe the difference between fun and joy to myself was that fun can bring laughter for the moment in which it is experienced; joy can often bring a tear from exultant happiness that is so intense that it is very satisfying and lasts forever. Once you have felt joy, you will always seek its company.

An old Chinese Proverb says, "One joy shatters a hundred griefs." You can laugh away a sorrow, but it will return. The joy you experience will remove your heartaches, pains, unhappiness, and all woes. Once you've had joy, you'll remember it forever. I have often thought that once you have reached a stage of true joy, you have fulfilled your purpose of life. Our work, then, is to find those who have tears of sorrow and help them to change them to tears of joy.

I called Martin the next morning and told him of the candy store idea. He grasped the concept immediately and said, "It just gets better!"

I told him I had Barbara working on a layout that wouldn't change existing plans and was told to get them to him as soon as possible. He assured me that management would jump all over it.

There were a couple of new stores in the mall that I would have to get familiar with, and I thought it important to reacquaint myself with all the other stores' offerings. It was fun visiting the managers and walking through their beautiful stores. Most of the managers said they were expanding their Christmas decoration this year because of the great successes they experienced last year. They were glad to hear that we were also planning greater things in the Santa Village, and agreed that the plans would probably bring many more people to the mall.

When I walked into the Toy Store, I introduced myself to one of the store representatives and was told not to go anywhere. "Mr. Henley said you would probably be coming in, and he wanted to meet with you personally."

Almost running, he hurried off and, in seconds, Mr. Henley appeared. A handshake wouldn't do, he indicated; I deserved a big hug. He said, "I was so happy to hear you were going to be our Santa again. Let me bring you up to date on the toys. This is going to be a fun year. We have a number of new toys and some that are returning because of their popularity."

We started with the dolls. "One of the favorites will be a monkey called Fur Real Monkey. We'll refer to her as 'Cuddles, My Giggly Monkey.' This monkey responds when you play with her. She giggles and makes monkey sounds when you cuddle or tickle her. Swing her in the air and she knows when she's upside down. When you put her to bed, she closes her eyes."

Mr. Henley next handed me a doll and said, "Give her a hug." I'll be darned if the doll didn't hug me back.

Mr. Henley then said, "There are a number of tablets available for children, but my favorite is the Kurio Touch 4S. Children can download many free games right off Google, play apps, and be entertained for hours."

He next showed me Zoomer the puppy. Zoomer was the solution for a child who cannot have a pet. He is a Dalmatian-like robot puppy that you don't have to wash or feed, but he will go for a walk in the park with you. It took a good hour to go through all the toys available, and it was done with much enthusiasm.

As we came to the end of one row of toys, there was a young man, probably in his late twenties, stocking shelves. Mr. Henley seemed to go out of his way to introduce him to me.

As we went on our way, Mr. Henley said, "That young man came to me for a job, which I didn't have at the time, but I hired him anyway. He is just finishing college, and I found from talking to him that his wife is going to have a baby just about Christmas time. Of course, I got the No-room-in-the-inn complex when I found they didn't have insurance for childbirth, and thus needed to make all the funds they could. I was told they have about $2,000 saved up now, but even with the money I can pay him, they are going to be far short of being able to pay for their baby."

The thought struck my heart, *This is one baby that isn't going to have to be born in a manger.* I said my goodbyes and thanked Mr. Henley for the great update on the toy availability.

He said, "I can hardly wait for Christmas to get here." It wasn't about money with this toy store owner. It was all about the joy he would see in those whom he served.

I went home and did some research on the cost of bringing a child into the world. The Internet let me know that prenatal care alone could cost almost $2,000, and that depending on how the birth went, hospital costs could reach anywhere from $9,000 for a natural birth to $20,000 if there were complications or if a caesarian birth had to be performed. And then there were the basic supplies that should be considered after the birth: car seats, cribs, diapers and wipes, some sort of a changing table, and a few baby clothes to get started. These were all considered necessities for a baby today, probably around another $450.

When I told Sarah about the young man and his wife, she said, "I don't know how kids can afford to have babies anymore. Even if they have insurance, there's still a lot they have to pay for." As an afterthought, she said, "I suppose there is a lot we could do to help them."

The worth of having elves now became more apparent to me at this time: I had someone to help me. I prepared a presentation for our next meeting, and when it finally arrived, I had become quite enthusiastic about the project.

After we had settled down and everyone was in place (it seemed that we gravitated to the same chairs around the table each time and my place was always at the head), we went over all agenda items. I informed them that Mark, the young man with the Mrs. B project, had called and given us the date of the assembly that would be in her honor. It would be on the Thursday before Thanksgiving, and we were all invited.

Barbara said Mark had been by to pick up the scroll and was thrilled at how it looked.

We made temporary arrangements to all be there, and then went on to the next item.

I was given several pages of Christmas jokes, stories and anti-dotes, and I told them we would go over them at our next meeting to determine their appropriateness. Barbara had completed the recommended layout for the candy store. I couldn't believe my eyes. There were about 25 different kinds of candy that were all very Christmas-oriented, contained in pots and jars and vases of all sizes—large and small, and designed to show the candy at its best. She had large drawings of candy swirls and canes with intermixed Christmas ornaments all over to enhance the candy-store effect. Each child would be given a little gaily-designed sack to put their three favorite picks in. All of this took up only about a five-foot space as the children walked out of the village. Santa could even have a piece when he wanted one. It was wonderful!

When we finally got to new business, I told them about the young couple who were going to have a baby. I laid the situation out to them and told them that the funds were not the problem. We had more than enough to cover what needs they may have. The problem is that we and they would be the only benefactors of giving such a gift. The whole community, or as many of them as could be involved, should have the opportunity to help. This would take a little more effort on our part, but the outcome would be worth it.

Mable's and Ann's minds were off and running, suggestions started pouring out, and of course they could make many of the items needed: baby blankets, wash clothes, some of the clothing, etc. Ann said, "Just let us know as soon as you know whether it will be a girl or a boy, and we'll get started right away."

I told them that I had decided to visit several baby stores to see if we could get various items donated. Even if they could donate half the cost, it would ease the burden.

Mable said, "Wouldn't it be wonderful if they could wrap their donation as a present and deliver it directly to the home themselves? Can you just imagine receiving all those presents just before Christmas?"

I thought a visit to their obstetrician and even to the hospital would be in line. We would make this a community Santa project.

Before I could go much further with the baby plans, I thought I should talk to the couple and gather information. I headed to the toy store where a young man was busy helping with a window decoration. I found out that his name was Jacob, and was surprised to find that his wife's name was Mary. How appropriate! I asked Jake, as he liked to be called, if I might come over to their home later that day when he was through with work and meet with both of them.

With somewhat of a quizzical look on his face, he said, "Sure."

I wrote down his address and was told they would be available in three hours.

I had time to run to the mall and show Martin the drawings for the candy shop. I showed him the pictures Barbara had produced, and he was amazed.

He then said, "When I presented the candy shop to management, they grabbed on to the idea and each one of them started making suggestions, so they feel that they are part of this great plan. The only thing, Santa, is that they have made it a lot bigger than you were suggesting. They want to take your waiting room in the back and make it into a much larger store area. When the children walk in, they will have the Willy Wonka effect. They will be greeted by the wonderful world of candy—all free. They're even thinking of hiring a candy elf to help the children with their choices!"

I thought to myself, *Mable is going to be ecstatic; it is all her idea!*

Martin interrupted my thoughts when he said, "What a great idea—Santa's Candy Store! People will flock to it. We also did a cost analysis: if each child takes three pieces of candy (and by the way, I like your candy sack idea), the total candy cost will be just over $1,500. Pretty cheap advertising, if I might say so. We would surely welcome any other ideas your group might come up with."

He added that the CEO of all mall operations asked an interesting question during their meeting: "Do you think that this Santa Claus of yours might give us other suggestions throughout the year? He comes up with some great ideas."

We then said our goodbyes, and I received a big thank you.

As I was driving over to Jake and Mary's, I started laughing a little to myself. Martin's suggestion, that we might help the mall with its year-around planning, began to tickle me a little. I thought, *Santa's Think Tank! We would probably be able to give the mall many great ideas, but it would also help our mission. Customers were coming to the mall at Christmas time because we made them happy. When a visit instills a degree of happiness in people, wouldn't they want to repeat that visit over and over? What we could do with Easter and Valentine's and the Fourth of July and Thanksgiving, etc., by just making these occasions a happier experience, would stagger the mind.*

I started to imagine the many options for giving mothers

true thanks for what they do for Mother's Day. People might start coming to the mall just for a boost of happiness, and if they leave happy, they may spread that happiness and thereby we will have become successful in what we are trying to accomplish. My elves will jump all over this one. If we get paid for it, great; if we don't get paid, it would be even greater.

When I arrived, Jake and Mary were waiting for me. I was invited into their apartment, which was typical of most college couples' abodes. It was tiny with furniture that didn't match, but it was tidy, organized, and well kept.

Jake introduced me to Mary as Santa Claus. He grinned a little and said, "I don't know your real name." I said, "That's close enough."

You never know how to handle a situation like this. Insinuating that they are down and out could be an embarrassment to them. They are just folks who have put their lives on hold while seeking to improve their status and abilities to contribute to society. It seemed like they were doing everything possible to make ends meet while all of this happened.

I said: "My, but this is like taking a trip down memory lane. I remember when my wife and I were trying to get through college. It's hard to determine how to make a life and get a degree at the same time; that's why I'm here.

I continued: "You're to be congratulated on what you're accomplishing. Sometimes, there are those who just want to help. It is not always because they think a person is destitute; it can be because they believe a person is deserving. I believe you are that type of people.

"Your plate is pretty full with a full-time job and trying to complete the last semester of your college career. You are certainly trying to do everything you can, but sometimes life presents a challenge, such as a little baby on the way. When you've done everything you can and it just doesn't quite get the job done, it's okay to rely on others to help. And those who want to help are often those who are acquainted with misfortune. They have learned the hard way, and want to help the less fortunate.

"We don't consider you the less fortunate; we consider you as the fortunate. So far you have made all the right decisions. You have chosen to get an education; you have chosen to start a family; and you have learned how to sacrifice. So we would like to help you so that you can continue on this path."

Mary stopped me here and said, "Are you the *real* Santa?"

I said, "What do you think?"

She said, "Well, if you look like a duck, and quack like a duck, you must be a duck."

I asked her when her baby was due, and if they knew what it was going to be yet.

I was told that it would come just before Christmas, and that it would be a baby boy. They were very excited and couldn't seem to wait for his arrival. But they confessed they were somewhat worried about taking care of all the costs that would be needed. Some of the costs the hospital would let them pay over a two-year period, but other costs needed immediate attention.

I said, "This is why I'm here. We would like to take care of everything needed to bring your son into the world."

They looked at each other and then back at me as if waiting for further explanation. I told them what Mr. Henley had told me—mainly that they had no insurance.

"Life is hard enough," I said, "when you start out on an even plane, but when you start out in a hole, it can just get too difficult. When someone has the means to help avoid this situation, he or she should take action. When one person in a society is made better by other persons in the same society, that society benefits greatly."

Jake said, "You keep mentioning 'we.' Are others involved?"

My response gave them no reason to ask further questions. I said, "Oh yes, my elves of course!"

Jake then said, "Let me get this straight. You mean you and your 'elves' are going to *help us* with the cost of having our baby?"

I said, "You are partly right. Only we would like to bear the *whole* cost of this child's birth."

He couldn't find the right words to say, but the words he did have were a credit to him and spoke well of his character. He said, "I have saved some money, and working for the toy store will help with a little more. We didn't plan to have a baby, but we know now that it was the right thing to do. We have such great faith in each other that we were sure we could work it out somehow."

I responded, "Your great faith is what has brought us here."

Mary had her hand on her tummy, holding her baby, and tears formed. Her expression was all we needed to move forward.

I gathered from them needed information—their obstetrician's name and address, the hospital where the delivery would take place, and what they had gathered in preparation for needs after the birth. I knew that other items would come up, and asked them to call if they thought of anything else.

Jake asked if they should just give us the money they had already saved. I told him that I wanted them to use it as a slush fund. There would be a few items we might forget or that they might need to replenish—and definitely they should get a few Christmas presents. I felt it important that they not only start out right but also have fun doing it. I then told them it would take me a few days to put everything in motion, but that I would keep them filled in on our progress.

As I was leaving, I looked a little longer than usual at Mary. The thoughts in my mind needed time to be brought to a conclusion. Here was a young woman who would change in a moment from a girl and wife to being a mother. There is no other time in her life that she would be as radiant as she was right now. Her whole person seemed to have a glow. She was being prepared for a miracle. I wanted to be Santa, but she would be a *mother*.

There was just too much going on. We needed an emergency meeting. I called my elves, and all but Barbara could make it. I let her know I would fill her in later. Ann and Mable came right over. Ann had been cleaning house and still had her apron on, and Mable was working in her garden and never bothered to take her gardening hat off.

Before we got into the main reason I had called this meeting—which was Jake and Mary, I told them of my meeting with Martin and the plans for the candy shop. They were ecstatic.

Mable said, "Whoever thought that a retired old lady could contribute to a major operation like a mall?"

When I told them about helping the mall year 'round, they had a hard time taking it all in. When I finally got to the main reason for calling the meeting, without even going into details, Ann said, "I think we might need more elves; we might even need professional elves."

I answered her by saying, "What is the difference between you and a professional elf, and where would I go to find professional elves? My elves are all experts in what they do. They are qualified and proficient and have been trained their whole lives for this work. You are even certified. There's nothing amateur about any of you!" I've always believed that if folks are told what they are qualified to do, they will do it.

We then moved on to Jake and Mary's needs. I filled them in on all the details and let them know it was going to be a little baby boy. After I got them calmed down from their enthusiasm, I asked if they could get together and make a list of what is needed to welcome a new baby into the world. Jacob and Mary told me they had a few newborn baby clothes and a couple of boxes of diapers, but that was about the extent of their readiness. There was a children's store in the mall that we could probably rely on for some discounts. I would approach them as soon as I could get a list of items needed. In the meantime, I would visit with the doctor and the hospital and let them know of our project.

I decided to go to the hospital first, since I was somewhat familiar with their operation. When I arrived, I went to the information counter, and they directed me to the financial department. I thought it important to talk to the person in charge so as not to have to be redirected several times.

I walked up to the receptionist and handed her my Santa Claus business card. I asked her who was in charge of the financial department, and was told it was Mrs. Bonnie Dalton. I then asked if I could speak to her. The receptionist took my card and disappeared down one of the halls.

When she came back, she was accompanied by a kindly looking lady. She introduced herself as Bonnie Dalton, director of the finance department. She said, "You are our Santa. Wasn't it you who visited our children last Christmas?"

I told her it was me, and that it was the highlight of all of my visits last year. Mrs. Dalton then invited me down the hall and into her office.

After a few niceties, she said, "I assume that this call is about your visit to our children this year, but why come to the finance department?"

After letting her know that I was there for a completely different reason, and assuring her it was strictly Santa Claus business, I went into great detail about Jacob and Mary's plight.

I told her that I knew the hospital operated under a business umbrella that had guidelines they had to follow, and then asked her if hospital policies could be altered in any way. I told her that Jacob had come in and arranged for a two-year payment program but that we had the funds and would be responsible for bills. We just hoped there was some way they could be lowered.

Not deviating from her business image, she smiled and said, "Well, Santa, a business like ours that deals with a whole lot of sorrow has to have a big heart. When a situation like this comes to us, we put it under the category of compassionate service. It has to be taken to a committee for discussion. If you will give us a one-page request with approximate dates, names, and addresses, we will do something. It goes without saying that we do appreciate what you are doing."

I told her I would return tomorrow with the proper request, and said my goodbyes.

As I was leaving, she said, "Mr. Harrington speaks very highly of you, and by the way, he is on the compassionate services committee. The committee meets every other Wednesday— which would be this Wednesday, so you should have your answer very soon."

I left the hospital not knowing exactly what to feel. I certainly had mixed emotions. I knew that there must be hundreds of young couples in the same boat as Jacob and Mary. And I also visualized all of the trauma that went on in a hospital and how many people could be given relief, or be supported or even rescued in so many different ways.

I thought to myself, *Where does our obligation begin and end when it comes to so great of a responsibility? How much of a difference can we make?*

There is so much need and so little help. I could see why so many get frustrated knowing how relatively little they can do—which sometimes causes them to do nothing.

It became very evident that there are just too many people in the world for one person to help them all. The beautiful thing is that we don't have to be exceptional to make a difference in the life of another. We all have the ability to make a difference; it may only be in one person's life, and it may be a small change, but many small changes add up to something bigger.

If I am not one who gives anything, and there are many like me, there will soon be no one who gives. Giving has to start somewhere. I somewhat phrased a motto out of all of this thinking: "For those I helped, I made a difference."

It reminded me of a story I had heard several times in my life, but is tender enough to be repeated: It seems that an older gentleman was walking down a beach and came upon a young man who was busy bending over and picking up starfish, and one by one throwing them back into the ocean. The old man, questioning his intent, made the statement, "Do you know how many miles of beaches there are, and how many starfish are lying upon them? Do you really think you are making much of a difference?" The young man picked up another starfish and, giving it a gentle throw into the ocean, replied, "I made a difference to that one."

I decided to hold off on my visit to the obstetrician. Maybe information gleaned from the hospital could help in also convincing him that we had a just cause.

# 36

## *My 65th Christmas*

At our meeting that night, the main subject was the new baby. I reported on my findings, and Mable, Ann, and Sarah had made a two-page list of items that would be needed.

Mable laid out a beautiful baby quilt she had been working on and said, "That's one item we can check off."

We then went through the list and deleted several more items because they insisted on making them themselves. Funds were allocated for materials, and it was determined that I would approach those stores providing baby products in the mall to enlist their help in the matter. I reminded everyone that next week would be the Mrs. B assembly. It was to be at the local high school at 2 p.m. and only one week later would be our first day at the mall.

How had Christmas come so fast? This would be my 65th Christmas, and although I looked back with great memories on the Christmases of my youth, they just seemed to get better year after year.

A simple thought came to my mind: *As man progresses, why shouldn't his Christmases also progress?* I had gone from a time in my life where there was virtually no television to where I could watch a different Christmas movie every night and only get through about a fourth of those offered during the season. Do you know how many great Christmas songs have been added to my selections? Of course they have to start Christmas earlier, just so they can have time to present everything offered. Along with more movies and more songs and television comes more comprehension of how to make Christmas better.

We have become experts on how to celebrate Christmas. Many of us have a list of movies we have to watch. I can't imagine a Christmas with all of its meaning without blocking out a special time to watch "A Christmas Carol" by Charles Dickens. I can remember going to the local department store just to look in their window and see all of the wonderful Christmas offerings. There would be electric trains and Santa's Village and sugar plum villages. Now, even as an adult, I wouldn't miss a trip to see the windows. They are so spectacular that they even move the imagination of an old man.

I truly believe that the reason for celebrating Christmas has also progressed. Our knowledge has become enhanced. I see people doing wonderful things. Their own needs are sacrificed for the needs of others. Young adults are more readily seeing that giving love brings much more enjoyment than giving gifts. They have to be a little more inventive, but the rewards are worth it.

Some are dissatisfied that Christmas is too commercial, but they shouldn't give up on it. It has survived many centuries. Its intentions are pure. You should love people and let them know you love them with a meaningful gift. Christmas has its own tenacity. It holds persistently to the idea that it is needed. If you don't believe this, try just one year to skip everything there is about Christmas in your life. Christmas has become the one day that holds all the rest of the days of the year together.

I loved being Santa because I loved Christmas. Even with all of its imperfections, we haven't found anything better as yet. I love a quote by Hamilton Wright Mabie, who said, "Blessed is the season which engages the whole world in a conspiracy of love."

Well, the next day I took the list of baby items and started visiting stores that carried these products. My first stop was at a large children's store that was next to the mall. When I asked for the manager, I was told that he was out on business and would be back in about an hour. I glimpsed around and saw that they carried most of the items I was interested in. I knew of a smaller store in the area and decided that I would pay them a visit.

The store was called Little Things Mean A Lot. It was privately owned, and I took a liking to the woman who owned the shop. It was the owner herself who greeted me and asked if she could be of help. I handed her my card and introduced myself as Santa Claus. She didn't appear to doubt me and said, "We would be pleased to help you Mr. Claus."

I had been searching for some amusing reply, but I had been accepted as Santa and would go on from there. I told her I had a special project involving a family that was going to have a baby, and I needed to get a few items. I handed her the list and she said, "It looks like they don't have much to start with." I then told her a short version of the story and could see that she was somewhat moved.

She told me she could help with most of the items and could direct me where to go for the others. She said her name was Emily Ann Spellman but that I should just call her Emily Ann. Jokingly she said, "Don't you make these baby things up at the North Pole?"

I told her that we kind of stick to toy making. We were off on the right foot. Her shop was beautiful. It was evident that she loved working with children. She then let me know that I wouldn't be paying the marked prices on the items and asked when I needed them. I told her somewhere around the middle of December would be fine.

She had a suggestion to make and said, "Being that you are Santa, this has to be a very busy time for you. Could I make a copy of your list and start putting items together for you? I'll have them all priced, and we'll make sure they are good products."

I thought that sounded wonderful and gave her the go-ahead. I was told I could come back in three or four days.

RICHARD ROBBINS

# 37

## Mrs. B's Reward

The week sped by, and it was soon Thursday. It was time to go to the school assembly. I had let Mark know that we would be coming, and he said he would save some up-front seats for us. Sarah and I picked up Mable and Ann, but Barbara had to leave from work, so she would meet us there.

We arrived a little before classes were dismissed for the assembly but were met by a very impressive young man as we entered the auditorium. He said, "You must be Santa."

I said, "You must be Mark." We shook hands, which turned into a hug and a pat on the shoulder.

He then said, "This must be your wife," and then jokingly said, "I assume then that these might be a couple of your elves," laughing a little.

"Are we that obvious?" Mable asked.

A bell rang and students began taking their seats. We were soon joined by Barbara. I had advised Mark not to introduce us, as it would just detract from the honor meant for Mr. B.

When Mrs. B entered the auditorium, Mark pointed her out to us. It was obvious that she was a woman of character. She joked around with a couple of students and sat near the end of the row in front of us.

After a few announcements and a Happy Thanksgiving wish, everything became very quiet as if all knew the significance of the moment. It was evident that the whole school knew the purpose of the assembly—that is, everyone but Mr. B.

The curtain was open on the stage, and two young men entered from the back of the stage and seemed to be having somewhat of an argument. One said, "Come on Joe. You know she loves me more than you."

To which Joe replied, "Jack, how can you say that everything she does is about me."

The other said, "Well how come just last night she stayed after school to help me with my homework?"

To which Joe replied, "Well that's nothing! She comes to my home to help me once in a while."

Just then another young man entered from the left of the stage and they stopped him. Joe said to him, "Bill, you are the student body president and know the people in the school about as well as anyone. Can you help us with an argument?"

Bill said, "I can try."

Jack laid out the dilemma: "There's a certain person in the school, and Joe thinks she loves him more than me."

Bill said, "Well, I guess it depends on who the person is."

Joe leaned over and whispered this blessed name into Bill's ear. They weren't ready for the answer Bill gave.

Bill let out a little laugh and said, "Neither of you have a chance. She loves me more than both of you put together. Recently, when I was voted class president, she was the first person to tell me how proud she was and took almost a whole hour just giving me advice on to how to do the job properly." His remark just complicated things more.

Just at that time, a beautiful young girl started across the stage. Jack said, "Let's ask Carly! Who knows best the thought of a woman than another woman?"

Carly joined them, and they were quick to get her opinion. She said, "It's not often that one person will love three others at the same time. Do I know this person?"

Once again the name was whispered into her ear.

She said, "This isn't possible; she loves me more than the three of you put together. She even helped me sew a dress for the last prom."

Bill said, "We've got to get to the bottom of this. I guess the only way to get the right answer is to ask her directly." He faced the audience and said, "You know who you are. Will you come up and tell us whom you love the most?"

From the back of the auditorium, a very beautiful young lady stood up and started making her way slowly up the aisle to the stage. As she got to where Mrs. B was sitting, she leaned over and whispered in her ear. Mrs. B nervously arose and was escorted to the stage by the young woman.

Joe took it from there. He asked, "All right, Mrs. B, put us at rest. Which one of us do you love most?"

Mrs. B, although overpowered by the moment, teared up a little but was all smiles and said, "All of you—equally!" As expected, a standing applause erupted from the student body.

Without a moment's hesitation students started to rise and walk up the aisle to the stage, and formed a line waiting to tell Mrs. B why they loved her. A large comfortable chair was rolled out, and Mrs. B was given her place of honor.

Each student in turn took her by the hand, and each started their comment with the words, "Remember when...."

The first boy said, "Remember when in the very first class I took from you, you asked the question, 'Do any of you know George Washington?' and I answered, 'not personally!' You said, 'Every class needs a comic; you'll do.'"

A young girl then took her turn at the mic and said, "I was a sophomore when I took my first class from you. Remember when my mother passed away? You were the first person to give me comfort. I'll never forget the words you told me. You said, 'Don't worry about death; it is actually a beautiful thing. Worry about life, making sure it is the one your mother would want you to live.'"

An older girl was next in line. Maybe 30 or so, she was a past student of Mrs. B's. Recognition was immediate and they hugged. She said, "Remember when I graduated and was thinking about which college major I should pursue—whether I should look to be a career woman or take courses to help me be a better mother? You told me that all knowledge was important. You said, 'It's how you use that knowledge that counts. Take the courses you like and fit them later into your life.'"

As some told their experiences with Mrs. B, others' memories were stirred and the line grew in size. It went all the way up the aisle. I suppose these testimonials could have gone on for several hours, and almost all wished they would have.

Nearing the end of the hour, Mark stepped to the stage and took his place at the podium. He apologized for having to cut short the testimonials but felt that we probably got the idea of the beauty of this woman. He said, "We have an award to give to Mrs. B, and would like at this time to present it to her to express our love for her."

Another young lady approached Mrs. B and presented her with the box containing the scroll. Mark explained that in the box was a scroll that contained a pledge made by every student Mrs. B had ever taught, and a signature attesting to the pledge of each student. Mark then said, "I would now like to read you the words of that pledge:"

**Dear Mrs. B :**

All people should have someone in their lives who cares about them! When that person is someone who has no claim on them, but helps when they have special needs anyway, it astonishes us.

When we can't figure out how to be useful or of service, but feel there is something inside of us—something more than we are doing, we need someone to tell us what it can be. We need someone who won't point a finger at us but one who will point the way.

You, for the last 35 years of your life, have pointed the way for so many students. Your service to us has been a service of love. We hope you have felt our love in return. We can pay you in gratitude, but we can pay you better in kind—somewhere else in our lives.

Therefore, we the students of Mrs. Burningham— our beloved "Mrs. B," pledge to you that as you have given freely of your love to each of us, and as we have benefited from that love, we will go forth from this day and for the rest of our lives share that love with all those whom we come in contact.

What you have given us, we will now give to others. We will refer to each occasion as a "Mrs. B moment." Our motto will be: "They who give, teach me to give."

Signed below by all of your students...

Mark then asked Mrs. B if she would say a few words. She stood and very calmly addressed the student body. Each person felt she was speaking directly to him or her. It was so quiet that it would have been hard to prove there were close to 1,500 students present. As she spoke, when she smiled, they smiled as a body; when she cried, they cried; and when she laughed, they laughed. There was no doubt that we were in the presence of greatness.

Mrs. B had never held a political position or written famous books or had ever involved herself in activities that had brought her notoriety. Not that she didn't have something great to offer; she just chose to spend her time with her students.

She said, "I've never been more than a schoolteacher. I don't even know another way of life. You are what brings meaning to what I do with my days. And it has been worth it. I have chosen to surround myself with young energetic people. You are my friends. Why wouldn't I want to see each of you do well in life? I have received nothing but kindness from you. Who needs more than that to live on? Am I sorry I have to quit teaching? Not really. You've about worn me out. But I've got a little life left in me—and what I have is yours."

She then walked back to her chair and sat down. The thought came to my mind: *She hasn't just given until it hurt; she has given until it made her feel better. The gift given was her very life.*

# 38

## Little Things Mean A Lot

Before heading home I checked my phone messages, I saw that Emily Anne from Little Things Mean A Lot had left a message. She said she had all the items gathered and could I stop by. I brought the elves up to date and asked if they had time on the way home to stop in with me.

When we arrived at the store, introductions were made and we were directed to a back room. The items were arranged so we could easily see them, and they were much admired. Emily Anne pulled out the list and went over each item. She let us know that there were many things not included on the original list. She also said that the items were not the top of the line but were very high quality, and would more than do the job yet keep costs down.

She added something I thought was insightful. She said, "You know, a mother is equipped with everything needed to raise a new baby."

She had made a new list and had broken it into categories. The first included layette and diapering. She said she wouldn't worry too much about these, as they were mostly given as gifts.

Ann and Mable then revealed to us that they had made crib-sized quilts, a beautiful light-weight comforter, washcloths, many receiving blankets, and a couple of swaddling blankets. Anne had knitted two newborn baby caps, and they had even thought to make several burp cloths, which reminded me of an old saying that I thought was humorous: "Out of the mouths of babes—comes mush."

I thought, *When did they have time to do all of this?* But the fact that they had done it was very gratifying.

Emily Ann had chosen a crib that could also be used as a changing table, a car seat that could also double for a stroller, and other items she thought essential. Off to the side was a box with assorted items in it—items I knew she didn't carry in her store. There was baby shampoo, a tube of diaper cream, baby nail clippers, baby oil and lotion, a little comb and brush, a couple of pacifiers, a digital thermometer, and a nasal aspirator. In another box were 12 four-ounce baby bottles with nipples, and yet in another box was a night light allowing for low light near where the baby slept so it could be checked on, or have its diaper changed without a lot of fuss.

Emily Ann handed me a bill to look over, and I was totally humbled by the amount. Every item was accounted for, and a note was made by each to explain the amount. It read, "Crib— donated by manufacturer" or "car seat—donated by manufacturer." Each item listed a local store or a person's name. When I got to the bottom of the bill, the amount was zero.

Before I could react, Emily said, "There are a couple of items that haven't arrived as yet. It's a rocking chair for the mother and one certificate for a three-months' supply of diapers."

I knew what would happen; Mable and Ann and Sarah were all just crying. Emily Ann finally lost her composure and joined them. I thought of the hours she had put into this effort. I learned a long time ago not to say to these givers, *Oh you shouldn't have done this.* Of course they should have. So I learned to say, in many different ways, "Well done."

Emily Ann said, "I hurried this project a little because half the fun of having babies is getting ready for them and arranging their little part of the world perfectly to greet them. Would you mind if I wrapped them all pretty for Christmas and delivered them myself as soon as possible? I'll tell them that Santa sent them over."

I told Emily Ann that I had been wishing she would say that. "You'll love this young couple, and the memory of your goodness will be accentuated for the rest of your life."

On the way home, the whole experience seemed to be more than Mable and Ann could comprehend. Anne said, "I thought we were being good sewing a few blankets and burp cloths."

I said, "Don't diminish what you have done by what others do. We each have various abilities. All you are asked to do is what you can do. It goes without saying that we can all learn from each other."

# RICHARD ROBBINS

# 39

## Good Hospital News

When I arrived home I checked my messages and saw that I had received a call from Bonnie Dalton. She left a message and said she had an answer for me concerning the aid to the young couple. I immediately called the number she left me, and it must have been her private number.

She answered, "Mrs. Dalton."

"This is Santa Claus. I received your message," I said.

She couldn't wait to tell me her news. She said, "It appears that when we don't have to go through an insurance company for payment, and when it is not necessary to work out extended payments, in other words, if we receive cash for the work done, we have the ability to offer rather large discounts. For example, in just such a case, the blood test that would have normally cost $415, we were able to discount it to $95 for a cash payment. Because there is considerably more work involved in a birth, the discount might not be as drastic but will definitely be as much as 50 percent. I will personally monitor this birth, especially if you will let me know when they come in and see to it that everything that can be done will be done in this case. Just remember, you will still have to come and visit our children again."

Loaded with this information, I paid a visit the very next day to Mary's obstetrician and received the same results. Sometimes, all you have to do is ask.

I called Jacob and Mary to put their minds at ease so they could enjoy this baby experience. I told Jacob that it was important to call me as soon as Mary was taken to the hospital for delivery, and with that, I put my mind to rest on the matter.

All I had to do now was concentrate on Christmas, which for me would start in less than a week.

# 40

## A Thanksgiving Kickoff

I had called Kate and asked her if she could meet me at the mall at 10 a.m. the next morning. She was right on time. We met at Martin's office and he took us down to Santa's Village.

Small final touches were being made, but it was even more beautiful than last year. We tested the stage microphones and Kate's backup music. She loved it. Martin had sent her over a disk with all the songs on it earlier so she could practice. The spotlights were perfect, and the roaming microphone worked properly. Instead of a gaily decorated wall that used to hide Santa's room, there was a window displaying the candy shop and a door for the children to enter. The candy store would have been a successful enterprise on its own. It drew you in and gave you so many choices.

It had been decided much earlier that another elf would be necessary, and Mable and Ann had insisted on making the costume. The elf would be dressed in candy cane striped leggings, with an apron and a chef's cap. She would have the hardest job of any of us—helping children limit their choice of three pieces of candy.

Kate had actually helped us find the right person. There was a girl she knew who had the Christmas season free and needed a job to help with her first semester costs of college. There was a scurry to get her measurements, make the costume, and do a fitting. Her name was Riley. She was delightful and loved children—the only qualifications really needed.

We felt confident that we were well prepared and that this time knew what to expect. We would be more alert to others' needs, and we were better prepared to take care of them. I could be Santa; I could exist as Santa; and there was nothing that Santa could do that I couldn't—even if it required a little magic. I wanted people to know that they could come to me for help and love.

As we walked through the halls of the mall, everything was more impressive than ever. Everything seemed to shout love and joy. Shopkeepers were stepping back and observing their own Christmas creations, satisfaction turned to fulfillment, fulfillment to joy, and joy to spirit—and the Christmas season was on.

I loved that we had a day of Thanksgiving right before Christmas. It gave me time to take a break in my life and consider what I have. I had found over time in my daily prayers that the asking parts were always much longer than the thanking portions. It probably should be just the opposite. Every time I thought of all the things I should be thankful for, it drew me into a meditation of whom I should be thankful to. It seemed that I could think of a person who deserved thanks for every material possession I have. As I pray nightly, I thank the Lord for all He has given me. Should I also thank each person for the part of my life she or he has enhanced?

I started to think of each person I know, and without question I could think of a reason that every one of them deserved some degree or another of a thank you for enriching my life. Thanks to each of these persons could certainly be made in my prayers, which would be good because it would remind me and the Lord of their goodness, but this could also be done in so many ways personally. After all, they are not there kneeling by me to hear my prayers.

For the numerous gifts given of a spiritual nature—those gifts relating to the soul, the gift of life, of nature, of joy felt from the heart and enriching the soul—I had to consider that they have a source and that this Source must be thanked.

The problem here is that these gifts are *assumed* gifts, those we think we have a right to receive. They are too often taken for granted. If I would just take some time to think where I would be without them—the sun, the rain, water, food, etc.,—they might be considered more deserving of daily thanks.

The Friday after Thanksgiving was the start of Christmas shopping. The reason I believe it is called "Black Friday" is because so much money is made on this one day that most businesses can move out of the red and into the black on their accounting books.

I also remember from my history studies that during the depression, President Roosevelt moved Thanksgiving up one week earlier so that the Christmas season could be extended.

RICHARD ROBBINS

# 41

## *Our First Day at the Mall*

Christmas seemed so much more effortless this year. The physical demand, as well as the mental, was less strained. It seemed to give me the ability to enjoy it more. I didn't have to stop to think what I should be doing now; everything came naturally. Is this what being felt like? It seemed that the more I did, the more I was. What I had done in the past and all I was doing now are what I had become to this point. The future just represents what I can be.

I was so excited for our first day, but when Kate arrived, she was so enthusiastic that my excitement went up several notches. We had a little room to relax in from time to time, and from there we would make our entrance.

Kate said, "Have you seen all the people out there?"

I opened the door a little so she could see them. If you think people are surprised when they see Santa, you should see how surprised Santa is when he sees that many people! There had to be at least double the number that there were last year.

There was a slight knock on the back door, and I was surprised to see Sarah and my elves standing there. They had come for a final check, and I invited them to stay with us as we made our grand entrance. Ann had brought a sprig of holly to pin on Kate's elf costume. It seemed to be just the thing that was missing, and final adjustments were made to Riley's costume.

I asked them if they could keep an eye on the candy store as children started entering—just for a little while to make sure everything was perfect. I knew it would be in good hands and didn't worry about it anymore. Riley looked wonderful. She got caught up in the spirit, and I told her to just have fun and of course help the children to have fun. Kate informed me that they had sung duets together before and that she had a great voice.

Just like last year, at ten minutes before 10 a.m., the mall sound system announced that Santa would be arriving in ten minutes. And then again at five minutes the announcement was made, and the crowd continued to grow.

Right at ten o'clock, the PA system announced, "Ladies and gentlemen and boys and girls, the Downtown Mall would like to present Kate the Elf!"

Kate opened the door and ran right to the piano and over her microphone said, "Boys and girls, let's welcome Santa with his favorite Christmas song, "Santa Claus Is Coming to Town."

She began playing, and the children and parents followed her as she sang, *"You'd better watch out...,"* and just then I opened the door, and hefting a very large bag full of toys I made my grand entrance, and started around the circle greeting each child.

I have to stop here to kind of give you an idea of what was going through my mind. I thought to myself, *This must be what it is like going to heaven—hundreds of beautiful faces, all perfect, totally honest and pure.* All you have to do is look at a child to know God exists.

As I touched their little cherubic hands, it was like touching heaven. Indeed, they were all a little piece of heaven on earth. Pablo Casals once said it better than I ever could: "The child must know that he is a miracle, that since the beginning of the world there hasn't been, and until the end of the world there will not be, another child like him."

Children are all unique, and all have something exclusive to give the world. I can teach them because they believe in me. They believe in me, for children are charmed because they want to be, and they allow it to happen. Children take no thought of the past and do not allow thoughts of the future to affect what they are doing presently. They live for the present moment, and all of their senses are used for their present enjoyment.

Somehow, we as adults get caught up and are allowed to share these pure, unblemished moments with them. Could this be the purpose of a child, to remind adults that what they are doing at any moment is the most important thing they should be doing at the time?

I finally got back to where I could sit on Santa's throne. The very first child to sit on my knee was a young four-year-old girl. She looked pleadingly into my eyes and said, "Santa, I have a problem. Can you help me?"

Of course, she had my total attention. There is nothing I wouldn't do for her; her wish was my command. I thought it remarkable that the very first child I held would need my help. I was ready for any task, no matter how large. I asked, "What's your name and how can I help?"

She said, "My name is Jillian, and my shoe came untied. Will you tie it for me, Santa?"

I thought to myself, *Well, we'll start out with the small problems, and work our way up.*

It wasn't long before Mable got my attention, and I snuck over to have a word with her.

She said, "There's a young boy who asked if he could take a bag of candy to his friend. He said his friend can't come to the mall because he has to stay in bed."

I asked Mable to take me to the young man. He stood in the middle of the candy shop and was just taking everything in. It made me aware that many children had never seen such a wonderful sight. I walked up to him and said, "Do you know who I am?"

With a big grin, he said, "Santa."

I said, "I wanted to come and help you pick out a wonderful sack of candy for your friend." I picked up a sack and, with his help, started filling it with a wonderful assortment.

When we had picked about ten pieces, he said, "Oh, he'll love this. Thanks Santa!"

I told him that I hoped his friend would get better, and get out of bed soon.

He looked at me and said, "He never gets out of bed."

I asked the boy who he was here with, and he said he had come on his own. I found out that he lived in a housing development adjacent to the mall and had just walked over. He told me that he had promised Jamie, his friend, that he would check out Santa and come back and tell him about everything he saw.

I said, "I'll tell you what, meet me right here in the candy shop at 6 p.m. and we'll take this candy over to him together. He can see Santa for himself."

I don't know if he was so excited that he didn't know what to do, but he just turned around and started running out of the door, and yelling back over his shoulder, "I'll see you at six!"

Mable had been watching the whole incident, and dabbed at her eyes. I asked her if she had time to run an errand for me, and got an excited affirmative. I sent her to the photo shop in the mall, and told her to buy a digital camera that a ten-year-old boy would not have a hard time using. I gave her the Santa credit card and told her to make sure the batteries were charged so the camera was ready to use.

She said, "I'll take Ann with me. She knows about these things better than I do." And off they went.

I went back to the children and had a wonderful time talking to them. It was hard to believe, but I didn't find one naughty child in the whole group.

I heard the piano begin to play and Kate started singing: *"You know Dasher and Dancer and Prancer and Vixen, Comet and Cupid and Donner and Blitzen, but do you recall, the most famous reindeer of all?"*

She then asked all the children to name the most famous reindeer of all, and they all yelled out "Rudolph!" And then without being invited, they all began singing *"Rudolph the Red Nosed Reindeer...."*

Children actually came on the stage and leaned on the piano, and Kate, while playing one-handed, shared the microphone with them. Every child knows how to sing. Some can't carry a tune, but they surely know how to unload it.

One little boy actually took the microphone, sang a line or two, realized what he was doing, and somewhat embarrassedly passed it on to the little girl next to him. She mumbled out the words *"how the reindeer loved him"* and handed the mic back to a very amused Kate.

After the song was finished, a young man came up to Kate and asked for her autograph. It made her whole day. When she came back the next day, she had a stack of pictures of her in her elf costume, all signed and ready to be handed out.

Mable and Ann came back with a wonderful camera. All you had to do was look on a rather large screen and push the button. You could then go back and review each picture you had taken on the screen. I gave the camera back to Kate and asked her to take a lot of pictures, and to even run down the mall and take pictures of the stores and the large Christmas tree, of Santa with his elves, and a few of the candy store.

I watched Kate throughout the day, and she seemed to be having fun, and used her imagination to capture the whole spirit that was part of Christmas.

By the time the day was over, I had reaffirmed in my mind why I wanted to be Santa. I guess part of being Santa is simply wanting to be him. But I perceived *wanting* as more than just a desire or an aspiration or even a fancy. I looked at it as though I was in want. Without the opportunity to serve and to love, there had been a deficiency in my life. The need I had felt to become Santa seemed greater than the need the children had for a Santa. Gladly, through this service, I had re-discovered the basic elements for a happy life.

Before Sarah had left with Mable and Ann, I had let her know that I would be a little later getting home. I hurried into the candy shop at 6 p.m. and, sure enough, the young man was waiting for me to take a bag of candy to his friend. I found out that his name was Eddie—Eddie Holmes. We got a lot of waves and "Hi's" as we walked through the parking lot and down a row of housing. We even had a small group of children following us. I had taken the camera from Kate, and managed a few pictures as we were walking down Eddie's street.

Eddie walked right up to a house and rang the doorbell. A woman, who I assumed was Jamie's mother, answered the ring, and Eddie said, "I brought Santa over from the mall to see Jamie."

She seemed to be used to almost anything from Eddie, and said, "Okay! Won't you please come in?"

I followed Eddie straight to Jamie's room and heard him say, "Surprise!"

Well, surprise was the least of Jamie's reactions. He was more in shock. He said, "Now I've seen it all. How did you manage this, Eddie?"

Eddie said, "It was Santa's idea, and he brought you a sack of candy from the candy store."

I pulled out the camera and dialed up a picture of the candy store and showed Jamie. He was amazed. After wishing Jamie a Merry Christmas, I told him that I had brought him and Eddie a joint Christmas present. I had put the camera back in the box and presented it to them. I said, "Since you can't get out, Eddie can take pictures of everything he wants you to see, and bring them back and show them to you. You won't be missing out on anything anymore. Eddie can take pictures of everything he does."

Jamie's mother said, "Eddie comes here every day and tells Jamie everything that is going on. You should hear some of the tales he brings back! He's a regular neighborhood gossip. It will be wonderful to have pictures to bring everything to life."

After taking the camera out of the box and admiring it, Eddie leaned down next to Jamie and took what he called a "selfie." Their bonding was made stronger.

After posing with the two of them and looking through the mall pictures Kate had taken, I left. I never did find out what was wrong with Jamie; it didn't seem important at the time. I wasn't about to break the spirit of the moment with a regression of what was wrong when everything seemed so right.

# RICHARD ROBBINS

# 42

## A Santa Solution

My increasing ability to recognize or perceive a person's needs may have been the reason there seemed to be more individuals requiring assistance this year. I may have also been more alert to such needs because of my increased capabilities—or means—to meet them.

On one occasion I had a little girl sitting on my knee, and I asked her if she was going to have a good Christmas. She said, "No, but Mother told me not to bother you with that."

Now, do I go against her mother's wishes and say, "Bother me with what?" or do I just let it pass and allow the little girl to have a not-so-good Christmas? I said, "Which one of those ladies is your mother?"

She pointed to a wonderful-looking woman, and I said, "Let's go get her and take her into the candy shop."

I introduced myself to her mother, and told her that I promised her daughter that I would take her into the candy shop. When we walked in the door I signaled Riley and told her to take the girl and help her pick out her candy. I told her to take their time doing it.

I then turned to the mother and told her what her daughter had told me—that apparently they weren't going to have a good Christmas, but that she shouldn't bother me with it. "I don't think you could come up with a reason that would disturb me or make me irritated or bother me," I said.

She thought on that for a moment and said, "I just don't like bothering people with problems that have no solutions."

I said, "Those are exactly the kind of problems you shouldn't have to face by yourself."

She reached into her purse and pulled out a Kleenex and dabbed at her eyes. She explained to me that her husband had died two months ago. He'd had cancer and couldn't be cured. The fact that I had caused her to bring this memory back made me wish for a moment that I hadn't bothered her. I said nothing to her concerning the matter; my own tears indicated to her my deep sorrow. She merely stated, "There's no solution for that kind of problem."

Not in a million years or in a million ways could I come up with a proper solution, and I had to recognize this. I thought to myself, *Sometimes we cannot make Christmas perfect, but there's never a time we can't make it better.* This needed some time for thought, which I didn't have at the moment. She seemed open to give me her phone number and address, and I told her that Santa wouldn't forget them this year. Her daughter's name was Amy.

I don't know how I could be so lucky—two years and two exceptional elves. Haley had swept me off of my feet, and now Kate was following her example. I had totally fallen in love with Kate's voice. It didn't matter if you were very young or very old because her way of presenting the story of a song was moving.

On one occasion, she gathered all the children around the piano and said, "I'm going to sing you a story about a very special night, a night when a baby was born. This baby was the most important baby to have ever been born in the history of the world, and His birth made this night a very holy night." She began singing "O Holy Night" and told us, through the song, that the stars were brightly shining and that this was the night the Savior would be born.

She went on to tell us that the world was having a lot of problems, but when the baby was born, each person felt His worth. The song went on to give us hope and thrilled us, and because of this baby, we felt joy. It reached a peak that overpowered us, and we felt thankful for this holy night. Every time Kate sang, a large crowd stopped to listen.

On another occasion, Kate hit a button on a recorder and the orchestration played the introduction to "Chestnuts Roasting on an Open Fire." She picked up a microphone and mingled with the crowd as she sang the song.

At one point, she noticed an older lady singing the words with her. She said she could tell she was a nice lady because all her wrinkles were in the right places. She went up to her and shared the mic. The lady had a beautiful voice, and Kate started harmonizing with her. As the song came to an end, the lady was totally caught unawares by the applause of those who had stopped shopping and had assembled to hear this rendering. Kate gave her a big hug and thanked her for her song.

The lady said, "Do you mean everyone heard us? Oh, I could have done so much better if I'd only known."

RICHARD ROBBINS

# 43

## The Token of Appreciation

One day before going to the mall, I received a call from the television station that had reported the Harrington story and the token of appreciation given last year. They wanted to make sure they would be given the opportunity to cover this year's story, and asked me if we had chosen anyone as yet. I told them we had two or three candidates we were considering, and we would definitely give them the story when it was finalized.

That night, after a day at the mall, Kate and I drove to one of our company parties. We had been to several parties and pretty well knew what we were doing. Kate's addition as a singer and a piano player was a great asset.

This party was for a very successful construction company that had built several housing developments in our community. The owner himself, a Mr. Clyde, had called and asked me to be their Santa this year. He had a reputation of building quality homes and always stood behind his work. It was a pleasure to meet this man. You didn't hear a lot about him in the community, but it was a better place to live because of him.

At the party, Kate and I had worked up a little duet that went something like, "Oh there's no place like homes, homes, homes and more homes for the holidays...." It brought a good laugh.

After we had finished our roles at the party and as we were leaving, a fellow approached us and said, "There is something you should know about Mr. Clyde." He went on to tell us about a very charitable person.

He said, "Mr. Clyde has now built 11 housing developments in our community. Every time he builds a development, he builds one extra house. It was always the model home. He has his own real estate company handle his sales, and his on-site salesmen collect stories of hopeful owners from their many open houses. There are many folks who come to the developments to just build dreams for the future—those who in no way could afford a home like this. And from these many home admirers, he chooses one and presents the home to them. The only thing they have to give for the home is a guarantee that they will never tell anyone of the gift."

It was easy to see the reason Mr. Clyde didn't want the community to know of his philanthropy. If they did, every time he built a development he would be inundated by folks looking for a free home. At all costs, such goodness must be protected. It also followed that his goodness in some way must be rewarded, as he had given homes to 11 families so far without receiving so much as a public thank you. He was certainly worthy of the Token of Appreciation.

No matter how long I thought or how many options I considered regarding how to present the token to Mr. Clyde, I couldn't come up with a way that would not, in some way, lead to the discovery of his generosity. I still believed he should receive some appropriate public recognition for his goodness, and I needed time to kick the idea around.

# 44

## Childhood Repentance

My thoughts and solitude were interrupted by a phone call. I found that all phone calls to Santa were good; this was one of the really good ones. When I said hello, a voice said, "Hi Santa. Have you missed me this year?"

It was Haley. I learned that she was home for the Christmas vacation. She asked how the new elf was, and told me her dad was very pleased with her. I found out about everything she was doing. She was living her dream. She was learning from the greatest musicians in the world and told me that she was playing the flute better than even she could have ever imagined.

When she said, "I wish I could play for you now," I said, "Why can't you? Come to the mall, and just for old time's sake, play for us."

She said, "Do you think Kate would mind?"

I told her that she had already expressed how much she loved to hear you play, and maybe you could even do something together.

She said, "I still have my elf outfit."

I told her to wear it if she wanted to.

"I'll be there the day after tomorrow," she said.

I couldn't wait to see her. Even more, I couldn't wait to hear her.

I decided to let Haley's visit be a surprise to Kate. I knew Kate wouldn't mind. All she could talk about at times was how great Haley was last year, and her wish that she could have met her. I did go home and give Mable and Ann a call and told them that they might want to be at the mall at 2 p.m. on Thursday, because there was going to be something very special.

Later, as I was sitting in my Santa throne, as we called it, I looked down at all the children, and there was one little fellow who couldn't seem to hold back his tears. He was making great attempts at composing himself, but just when he seemed to have it under control, the sobs began again. It seemed the closer he got to his turn with me, the shorter his controlled periods became. I had so much compassion for him that by the time he got to me, sobbing uncontrollably, I gathered him in and said, "You're not afraid of Santa are you?"

It all came out in one long sentence, and so fast that I had a hard time understanding him. He said, "I've been naughty. I pulled the arms off the doll you gave my sister last year, and felt so bad that I just hid it, and she hasn't had her doll for a whole year!"

To him, this was a very serious problem—one he didn't know how to deal with. His sorrow and remorse were heartfelt, and he was contrite to the point where he would listen to almost any advice. I wanted to make sure his sorrow was for the right reason, so I asked him, "Do you think that you have been naughty enough that Santa shouldn't bring you a present this year?"

He put it very simply in his reply, "I don't think that I should get one."

I just couldn't let his heart break any longer. I asked him if he thought a bad boy would ever tell what he had done wrong, and he said, "Probably not."

I then said, "Would a good boy feel bad about what he had done, and finally tell someone?"

He answered, "Yes."

I said, "You must be a good boy, then."

His first smile appeared, and it was worth the effort. But we weren't finished. I asked him if there was anything else a good boy should do to make things right. He answered that he should probably tell his sister. I suggested that he might tell his parents first, and then together they could tell his sister. I told him that the main thing he had to do was to tell his sister that he was sorry, and then ask if there was anything else he should do to make things right.

I could tell that he had thought this through earlier, and it was probably the reason he came to me in the first place. He said, "Could you still give my sister what you are going to give her this Christmas, but then instead of giving me anything, could you give her another doll?" It was now Santa's turn to cry.

The boy had done his homework, and told me that the exact same doll was still available at the toy store. I called Kate over, and asked her to accompany this young man to the toy store and help him buy the right doll. I told her to just ask for Mr. Henley, and gave her the Santa credit card.

This young man had come to the mall with his mother, and he pointed her out to me. While Kate took him to the toy store, I approached his mother and told her the whole story. By the time I told her that she had a fine young son, she was in tears also. I said that tears must run in the family. I suggested that the doll be given to her daughter once her son told his sister that he was sorry.

As though she had had a revelation the mother said, "This must be why he has treated his sister as if she were a princess, all year long."

RICHARD ROBBINS

# 45

## A Company Party

Our company parties continued to be successful. We had several new companies through referrals from those we went to last year. We did our early investigations into each company, and designed our programs to fit their particular personalities. Adding Kate to our program was a stroke of genius. She had the natural ability to entertain.

One of the parties we were attending was a good example of her abilities. She asked the head of the business to come up and sing a Christmas song with her. Of course, with all of the employees' urging, he couldn't refuse. She asked him what he would like to sing and added don't say "Far, Far Away." He chose, "We Wish You a Merry Christmas" and began to play. He got as far as the first verse and couldn't remember the rest.

Kate said, "We need someone to help him," and several hands went up. She told them all to come up, and about eight people joined him. She said, "Let's start from the top, and don't hold back. He needs a lot of help." Then she started playing the song again. Whether they volunteered because they knew the song or just liked to sing, or maybe even to make points with the boss, the group sounded great, and even had some good harmony.

When they finished, there was major applause and Kate said, "Would you like to hear them again?" After a positive confirmation, she asked the rest of the group to choose the next song. They chose to sing "Chestnuts Roasting on an Open Fire." Four or five others rushed up to join them, and they weren't far into the song before the whole company was singing. Kate didn't have to ask for another song as requests just kept coming in. She ended by singing them "Merry Christmas, Darling."

It just so happened that one of the younger female employees had come up to join the singing group. I had been told secretly that she was still single. So I took her by the arm and said to the group, "This young lady came by the mall the other day, and I'll never forget her for her unselfishness. When I asked her what she wanted for Christmas, she said, 'Don't worry about anything for me. I just want something for my mother.'"

I told her I thought that was very thoughtful, and asked, "So what do you want me to bring her?"

Without blinking an eye she replied, "A very handsome and rich son-in-law!"

# 46

## Haley's Surprise

When I awoke Thursday morning the first feeling I had was anticipation. I knew that I was merely imagining, in advance, the pleasure I was about to participate in. I felt as though I was about to present to the world an experience that everyone should be able to participate in.

You see, I knew my elves well; I knew the hearts of both of them, and I knew their abilities. I knew that when you put Haley and Kate together—even without a rehearsal, but just with their love for music and wanting to share it, something special would happen. I had let Martin know about Haley's visit, and he had told others.

Just before 2:30 in the afternoon, I noticed that Mable, Ann, and Sarah had taken their places in the crowd. There seemed to be a lot of unknown faces to me, and more adults than usual. I went to Kate and asked if she could go out and sing two or three songs to get us in the spirit. She went straight to her piano, and the music started.

Haley had slipped in through the back and was in full elf costume. I hugged her as though she were one of my own. Without a word she opened her case and took out Freddie. I thought, *Freddie the flute, what joy you have given me!*

With a hushed tuning Haley was ready to go. Just as Kate started on her second song, "What Child Is This," Haley stepped out and joined in with what sounded like an angel's accompaniment from heaven.

Kate turned to Haley and a big smile came across her face, but she never skipped a note. Haley returned her smile, and with a nod they continued their presentation, devoted in their desire to please the group.

Have you ever experienced perfection? It is an excellence, a faultlessness, just a rightness—something that in that moment could not be improved upon. And you as the recipient, you are perfectly fulfilled, nothing wanting. Such was this song, so divine in its presentation that applause would have been out of place.

It was Haley who broke the silence with a lone introduction to "Silent Night." The crowd of admirers let out a collective sigh, indicating their tender gratitude. Over Haley's flute obligato, in a voice so clear that it could have been mother Mary singing to her baby, and with no piano, Kate's soothing tones floated in perfect synchronization. Flute and voice carefully unfolded this first story of Christmas.

After the first verse, the piano seemed to come back to life and introduced the second verse, which was then turned back over to flute and voice. How did they know that this was what was supposed to happen? What internal instincts directed their presentation? It was as though they knew from some unknown source that it was just the thing they were supposed to do.

I noticed that no children were coming up to Santa. They were taken by what was happening.

After the song finished, Kate took the microphone and introduced Haley as last year's elf. They all seemed to remember her and she received a hearty applause.

I wish Haley and I could have taken some time to sit and talk, but for now we had a job to do. Santa's kids needed him. I did hear Haley tell Kate how great she was, and that she would stay for a while and they could play again. Haley's growth was evident; her year at the music school had matured her both in nature and talent. I thought, *How could she get better than she was last year?*

Throughout the day, we had many opportunities to talk and share meaningful experiences. Haley and Kate played several wonderful songs together, and neither seemed to want the day to end. Every time they began to play large numbers of people would stop to listen.

I loved the music. The only thing I loved more was the spirit of the day.

# 47

## Leap of Faith

I had for some time now, put writing paper and a pen on the night stand by my bed. I was always having thoughts that, if I didn't record them, would be forgotten by morning. Some of my best thinking was in the moments just before sleep took me away. I often thought that when all of my other functions were voluntarily shutting down, it caused less demand on my brain, and it could function separately in its thinking mode.

Sleep has always baffled me. Where we go for those few hours is a mystery. We just stop existing, or at least we alter our consciousness. I did know, however, that when I had a problem, getting to sleep was prolonged.

One recurring problem was hampering me lately from getting much sleep. I had to decide who would be chosen to receive the Token of Appreciation Award. I had strong feelings that it should be Mr. Clyde, but still could not come up with a way to present it without disclosing why he was receiving it— thus spoiling his desire to remain anonymous.

I took a leap of faith—faith that I could come up with a proper presentation, and called the trophy shop in the mall and told them I was going to need another Token of Appreciation award made. I was told that they could get the ball rolling, and when asked for the name I wanted engrave on it, I told them "Wilford Clyde." I told them I would get them the exact text by tomorrow. I figured I would need the day to come up with something proper.

I had about an hour before I had to start getting ready for the mall. Sarah recognized that I had something on my mind, and brought a plate of breakfast into the office for me. I started writing notes of what I wanted to say. After several attempts and searching for proper words, I came up with what I thought might be acceptable. It read:

> *"This Token of Appreciation is presented to Mr. Wilford Clyde who, through his care and consideration, has provided many quality homes for our community.*
>
> *His attention to detail, and revisits to each homeowner to make certain everything is acceptable, has endeared and deeply indebted us to him.*
>
> *This token also recognizes his many anonymous gifts— given not out of obligation, but out of kindness.*
>
> *Thank you, Mr. Clyde. We are a better community because of you."*

I would have Barbara design a companion letter describing the purpose of the token and its history, short as mine was.

# 48

## *Annual Christmas Hospital Visit*

I had contacted the hospital earlier to let them know the date of my visit to the Children's Ward. I was told they had plenty of presents and had sorted them out, not only by boy and girl, but by ages. This night I would have no company parties. I had found I could use all the time available to visit with the children. I couldn't—and didn't want to anyway—talk Kate out of coming with me.

When we arrived, Bonnie Bates from the billing department was there to greet us. She said, "A lot of our adult patients have heard of your visit to our children." I loved the way she referred to them as "ours." "They feel somewhat left out that they don't get a visit," she said."

Of course nothing would suit me better. Two reasons I hadn't thought about this myself were time, and access to adult patients. When I told Bonnie of my concerns she said, "You make the time, and we'll arrange the access."

The reactions from the children at the hospital were what I expected. Most of them were in very high spirits; others were just too hurt or too sick to make a big fuss. You can tell, however, that they were still glad we were there; the movement may have gone out of their little bodies, but the light never goes out of their eyes. Some of the parents who had heard I would be there gathered, and each waited to see Santa visit with her or his child.

I went up to one little boy's bed and, after giving him a big hug and receiving one back, I noticed he was missing one arm just above the elbow. I sat on the edge of his bed and said, "You must be a very brave boy. I see that you are missing your arm, but you have a very big smile on your face!"

He didn't say anything, but with a serious face and a fixed chin he gave a large nod of his head.

I asked him if he was excited about Christmas coming, and got two or three more nods back. I then asked if he knew what he wanted Santa to bring him for Christmas, and with his good hand he pointed to his missing arm.

It was not hard to tell which parents were his. They had inched a little closer to be able to hear, and the mother had a tear in her eye. I looked over at the father and he gave me a positive nod.

I turned back to the boy and said, "I believe I remember that we have an arm that will be just right for you. It was made by one of Santa's special elves. Can you imagine having a special arm made just for you, from Santa?"

Before leaving the hospital that night, I met with the boy's parents and learned that he had lost his arm in an automobile accident, and that they indeed intended to make sure their son had a proper prosthetic arm before leaving the hospital. They told me however, that their insurance would only pay the full amount for a purely cosmetic arm, or that they themselves would have to pay 20 percent of the total cost for a functional arm that ends in a split hook, or 30 percent for a micro-electric arm controlled by muscle movements—with a functioning artificial hand.

I was told that by the time they had paid the co-payment amount for hospital costs, they were afraid that they would have to settle for just the cosmetic arm. But I was assured that they would acquire a better prosthesis as soon as they could. I knew that it is much easier for a child to adapt if a prosthesis is used as soon as possible.

They had done their homework on costs, and a microprocessor battery-operated arm would cost approximately $20,000, leaving them with a 30% co-pay of nearly $6,000.

They had all been in the vehicle at the time of the accident, and the father still wore a bandage on his head from his injuries. It was a no-fault accident due to weather, but it's hard not to take the blame as the driver when a family member is injured. Here was a father who probably felt as bad as a dad ever could, and then felt even worse because he wouldn't be able to provide the best help for his son.

Putting yourself in the parent's shoes, you could somewhat imagine their reactions as I told them that Santa and his elves would like to take care of the cost of the arm. The mother almost passed out and had to be steadied by her husband. Although it hadn't fully sunk in yet, the relief on the father's face was as though he had been given a reprieve from a death sentence. I gathered the information I needed and took my leave of this very grateful family.

I had many wonderful conversations with the hospital children, and gave each of them a couple of Christmas gifts. One little girl didn't want to open hers yet. She wanted to save hers for Christmas morning. When asked why she wanted to wait, I was told that these were probably the only presents she would get, and that she wanted to have something to open Christmas morning. I told her I knew that she would be getting many presents, and that she could open hers now.

I then called Kate over, gave her a pad and a pen and said, "Kate, this is Tracy. Could you help make a list of presents this little girl wants for Christmas, and make sure you get her name and address?"

I didn't have to talk to Tracy's mother. I knew their story. It is repeated over and over again, and the cost of recovery just doesn't leave anything for Christmas. A real Santa would, of course, see to it that this would never happen, and I had elves who could help. Our needs list had grown much larger than last year's, but our resources had also increased. We had been blessed to become more proficient and competent in our work.

Realizing that I wouldn't have a lot of time, Bonnie had chosen a few adults who might benefit from a visit with Santa. I found their needs weren't too different than the children's, and after all, they were just grown-up children—my children.

My first visit was with a beautiful elderly woman. She perked up a little when I entered her room. She said, "I suppose you've come to ask me what I want for Christmas?"

I answered her that this was one of my intentions. She was 82 years old, and told me that she was going to be slowed down because of a back operation. She had the fear that before long she would be placed in an assisted living care center, and then be of no use to anyone.

One of the ironies of old age is that once you have lived a long life, and gained experience and knowledge that would allow you to be of great service to others, your motor abilities slow down, and others start to think you are less useful.

This lady said what I've heard too many times before: "Even my own children are so busy with their own lives, they don't have time to visit me. And I can't blame them. After all, they have lives of their own to live. They don't even come to me for advice anymore."

I loved her name, *Elizabeth*. It denoted wisdom and understanding. I said, "Elizabeth, can we not talk for a moment about what is going to happen in the future, but what has happened in the past? You appear to me to have lived a very wonderful life. Everything about you conveys a very full and inspiring past. Am I wrong?"

Her eyes seemed to focus on another time, and she acknowledged that she had had an almost perfect, idyllic life. Each phase—her childhood, her school years, her marriage, and her raising a family—couldn't have been better.

I said as calmly and reverently as I could, "Elizabeth you are merely entering another phase of your life: old age. The only way we can escape it is by dying when we're younger. And most of us don't like that alternative. I think this phase of your life can be as meaningful and full as all of the other phases. You had to change as you entered each of the previous seasons of your life to make them productive. Now all you have to do is change once more.

"This old-age phase requires you to slow down; it doesn't require you to stop. In fact, all you have done your whole life is now culminating at this time. You have reached the highest degree of your life, and old age is simply climaxing.

"This time is your time. You deserve it, and you require it. All of your past life has prepared you for right now. Why do you think we wait to die until we have aged? I like to think of it as the Grand Finale. How we go out is as important as how we came in. Usually, the best part of any performance is the end.

"Just as you were prepared to move to each new stage of your earlier life, you must have this current period of preparation for the last phase. This is probably why we're slowed down a bit—so we will have time to ponder and prepare and finish.

"I remember when I finished high school that I didn't want it to end. It was a wonderful period of my life. But when I started college, I was amazed at how fulfilling it was. In high school, I learned how to learn; in college, I learned how to live.

"The next step for you is the final graduation. It is the one step that is worth all the effort we have had to make on this platform called *earth*, a stage for our final performance. I want you to walk off of this stage with the audience clapping for an encore; but we must remember that there are no encores. We have learned how to live here so that we can then go on and in fulness live there.

"This life, then, is a time to prepare you to *live*. You don't start to really live until after your 'death.' How we live when we go on depends solely on how we lived while we were here."

"Elizabeth," I said, "you are bright enough to make this the best phase of your life, and to prepare well for the final and lasting season."

Elizabeth was smiling now, and that was all that was needed to assure me that she would be all right.

I asked if I could come back the day before Christmas and visit again with her, because there was something I wanted to give her, and she sweetly blinked her eyes and nodded yes.

RICHARD ROBBINS

# 49

## A Special Last Mall Day

I had Ann and Mable reading the children's letters from the post office. They would call and would either be laughing or crying as they read them to me. Mable called one day and said, "Listen to this: 'I will know that there is not a real Santa if my brother gets any Christmas presents. He has been very mean all year long.'"

Ann read another letter to me through a flood of tears. It read, "Dear Santa, Could you please bring something that would make my family happy? We are a very unhappy family. My mom is sick all the time. My dad is very worried about her. We were happier once."

I told Ann to think of something that would make them happy. We had their address, and her name was Mindy—Mindy Crandall.

The Sunday before Christmas we had Ann, Mable and Barbara over to dinner. Because we couldn't meet otherwise—as I was always involved one way or another in Christmas activities, we decided to take just a few minutes to make sure everything was completed to make Christmas happen on Thursday.

As we were eating the phone rang, and I could see that it was a call from Jake. He very excitedly told me that they were at the hospital and that Mary was in the delivery room. Everything had happened so fast, and this was the first chance he'd had to call me.

I told the group, and our first inclination was to pile into the car and head to the hospital. On second thought, we asked Jake to call us and let us know if everything was all right.

One of the most sacred occasions in people's lives occurs when they have a baby. Although there is much excitement for all involved, I believe firmly that a couple should have quiet time together to just share with each other this blessed moment. A miracle has happened, and there must be time for a new mother and father to enjoy the spirit associated with the moment. When I mentioned that we wouldn't bother them at the hospital, I was told they would be home Christmas Eve, and would there like to show us their beautiful baby. I told him we would be there—"we" meaning "me and my elves."

Monday morning I called the Clyde Construction Company and was able to talk directly to Wilford. I introduced myself as Santa Claus, the same one who was at their Christmas party, and he said, "What can I do for you, Santa?"

I asked him if I could come over on Christmas Eve and meet with him and his family. He said, "Are you available about two o'clock that afternoon?"

I told him I was.

He said, "Could you meet me at my Edgemont Home Development? I have a little business to conduct, and then we could go over to the house together." He said, "I believe Santa would be a nice touch for what I want to accomplish."

I told him that it would be nice to have his family at his home when we came over. I called the TV station and the newspaper and told them to meet us at the Clydes' home about 3:30 p.m.

I left home and drove over to Ann's. I gave her Tracy's Christmas present list and asked if she and Mable could run to the mall toy store and have Mr. Henley help pick up the items listed. They were thrilled with their assignment, and let me know they would have it completed today.

Mable was there when I later went back to Ann's. Unbeknownst to me, they had set up one of Ann's spare rooms as a Christmas-present wrapping room and they were busy wrapping receiving blankets, burp rags, bibs, and other items they had made themselves.

I arrived at the mall for our last day, as Christmas Eve was a day we did not work. Kate was already there and was ready for business. People had started pouring into the halls, and we could tell it was going to be a very busy day.

Kate told me that some of her friends were coming by today, and asked if I minded if they sang a few songs with her. She said that these were all singers from her music class at school. I never could have imagined the treat I was in for.

We had a fun day with the children. The closer to Christmas, the more excited they got. One little boy, with wonder in his eyes, and after staring questionably at me for some time, asked, "What is it like to be Santa?"

I replied, "What do you think it must be like?"

"It must be a lot of fun," he answered.

I asked, "Why do you think it is fun?"

"Because you're always laughing and giving presents and making people happy," he said

I said, "Anyone can do that—even you. You can always laugh and give presents and make others happy, so you must know what it feels like to be Santa."

"Wow! I could be a mini-Santa!" he exclaimed.

I said, "Every time you laugh or give a present or make someone happy, you become Santa's helper."

He jumped off my knee and let out a holler, "Hey, Mom, I'm Santa's helper!" running into the arms of his happy mom. He had already started as a Santa's helper.

That afternoon about a dozen young people joined Kate on her stage. The girls admired her elf costume and, after hugs, gathered around the piano.

Kate ran over to me and said, "These are the kids I told you about. You are going to like this!" Then, she ran back to her piano.

I noticed that Mable had gone back to the Candy Shop and Riley had joined the singers. Kate played one chord, and the song burst forth:

> *Go, tell it on the mountain, over the hills and everywhere,*
> *Go, tell it on the mountain that Jesus Christ was born.*

It was sung with full volume and in perfect harmony. They meant to get attention. A young man with a deep bass voice then started to sing, with humming behind him:

> *Down in a lowly manger the humble Christ was born*
> *And God sent us salvation that blessed Christmas morn.*

The chorus was then repeated in unison, after which Kate took the solo:

> *While shepherds kept their watching over silent flocks by*
> *    night,*
> *Behold throughout the heavens there shone a holy light.*

This time they began the chorus very softly but excitedly, and started the build up for the climax at the end:

> *Go, tell it on the mountain, over the hills and everywhere,*
> *Go, tell it on the mountain that Jesus Christ was born.*

After repeating the chorus a second time, building to a tremendous crescendo, it sounded as if they were truly shouting from the rooftops that Jesus Christ was born. And then in a feeling of wonderment, they ended very softly, *"...that Jesus Christ was born."*

By the time they finished, the halls of the mall were filled with people who had stopped to hear this message. Several of the singers had moist eyes as a rousing applause grew from what could only be called the Holy Chapel of the Mall.

Of course they would sing another and another and another as the crowd grew even larger. Martin was making his way through the crowd and around to the back of the setting. He very enthusiastically said what was becoming one of our favorite statements, "Well Santa, you've done it again."

I said, "Martin, this should become an annual event."

As the chorus started another song Martin said, "Isn't it fun to watch them? They sing as though they really enjoy it."

"They would sing all day if you let them" I responded.

After they had finished singing a rendition of "Chestnuts Roasting on an Open Fire"—that had everyone singing along, one of the young men went down into the crowd and coaxed a little girl to come to the stage.

He said, "I was watching you while we sang the last song, and you knew every word."

She gave out a little giggle.

He asked her what her favorite Christmas song was, and was astonished when she told him. He thought she might say "Jingle Bells" or "Santa Claus Is Coming to Town" or "Rudolph"—something in keeping with her age. But when she said, "O Holy Night," he, as well as the rest of the singers, dropped their jaws.

He asked her if she knew that song, and she nodded yes.

When he asked, "Would you like to sing it for us?" he was expecting some shyness, but she said, "I would love to, will you sing it with me?"

He told the girl that there would be an introduction in the music, and he would then point at her every time she should start singing.

Kate began playing this sacred song on the piano, and the singers hummed a perfect introduction. The young man pointed to her, but the girl already knew just where to come in and start singing.

Her voice belied her age as she shared with us a night when the stars were shining brightly. It was not only a holy night, it was also a night divine—the night that our dear Savior was born. As she sang on you were almost compelled to fall on your knees. We were hearing the angels' voices, and it infused us with hope.

She finished her song, but the applause was delayed. The shoppers were waiting and hoping for more—another verse, but this was all she knew. A couple soon started clapping, and the applause grew to a level where you knew the praise was heartfelt. It was one of those rare times when everything came precisely together to develop a perfect instance in time. Such may never again be repeated—at least not in its innocence.

Martin asked Kate and me to come up to the corporate offices before we left for the day.

Kate's friends had now left, and she was at the piano playing Christmas songs in a very melancholy manner. I said, "You seem a little sad."

She said, "This will be our last time."

I told her that it is never fun when a good thing has to come to an end.

She looked back at me with pleading eyes and said, "Does it have to end?"

I replied: "As long as you keep singing and making others happy, it will never end. In the entertainment business we don't call things *ends; we call them finales.* And how good your finales are will determine your number of encores. As long as you keep making people happy they will keep applauding—and you will never have to really *end.*

Kate and I closed down Santa's Village and wandered slowly to the corporate offices. People along the way shook our hands and wished us a Merry Christmas.

What is it about those two words that seem to have been designed to be said together, *Merry Christmas?* Christmas, the greatest of all days, should include all the facets of merriment, joy, gaiety, happiness, laughter, liveliness, bliss, exultance, delight, cheerfulness, gladness—and even content. I love that phrase every time I hear it.

At last we arrived at the corporate offices, which were highly decorated, and as we walked in people seemed to pop up from behind desks, cubicles, and every other fixture that could hide them—even plants. Curiously, they all began to clap as we entered. It took us a while to realize that the applause was meant for us. I stepped back and Kate took a deep bow, and then I gave my Santa wave.

Martin and the management team then stepped forward and handed us our pay envelopes, and presented each of us with a large Christmas-wrapped box that I found out later was the finest chocolates the mall had to offer. Santa would definitely weigh more next year.

After wishing them all the best for Christmas, I reflected that another year was now over at the mall.

RICHARD ROBBINS

# 50

## *Christmas Eve Day*

I awoke very early on Christmas Eve morning. This was going to be a very busy day. But it was not as if we had left everything to do until today. It was just that everything we had to do would have more meaning if it was done on Christmas Eve.

Thank goodness I had the elves to help. I still had to deliver each item, but they could have them all ready for me, and on some occasions even accompany me. Long before Barbara even got involved, she had planned a trip to be out of town for the holidays. It was her first vacation in several years, and we encouraged her to go.

After cleaning up and having breakfast and organizing myself, I dressed in full Santa apparel and headed out the door. My first stops would be at the hospital and then the OB/GYN office. I wanted to be able to present Jake and Mary a Paid-In-Full bill for Christmas.

When I arrived at the hospital I went directly to Bonnie Dalton's office. She greeted me and said, "I've been expecting you and have your bill ready. Please come in."

She told me she loved the Santa suit. I sat at her desk and was handed a bill for just $2,000. I was stunned. She said, "We managed to shave a little more off."

I thought a thank you was not nearly enough so I stood up, walked around her desk, and gave her the best Santa hug I had.

When I pulled away, she had tears in her eyes, and told me that several employees had made unsolicited contributions when they heard the story.

I told her that this happens often because people are basically very kind, and asked her to please give them each a hug. I gave her my Santa debit card and she ran it, and then marked the bill *"Paid In Full."*

I hadn't had much interchange with the obstetrician, but went to their front desk and told the clerk that I was there to pay the bill for Jacob and Mary's baby. She advised me that the doctor would like to see me. I was invited into her office, and it wasn't long before I was joined by Dr. Carol Graff.

She asked if I was the Santa who had been working with Mary and Jacob.

When I told her I was, she said, "After you stepped in to help, we noticed many significant changes in Mary. We wanted to thank you for putting them at ease."

I told her they had spoken very highly of her, and thanked her for being there for them. She then reached across her desk and handed me her bill; it was marked *"Paid In Full."*

I reached into my wallet and handed her the debit card and said, "This will cover what you charge."

She said, "It has already been taken care of."

I assured her that we didn't expect her to not be paid for her services.

She said, "Their baby came very close to Christmas Eve, so I thought it would be great every Christmas Eve from now on to be able to think back on this one particular infant as my gift to the world. I know it's not much, but it would make my life more meaningful."

With a growing sense of wonder, I graciously accepted her gift and took my leave.

That morning I had assigned my elves to go to the grocery store and pick up everything that was necessary for a fine Christmas dinner. I told them to put the food in bags and tie a nice Christmas ribbon around them. I returned home, and they had everything ready.

We loaded the dinner items and many toys for Amy. We wanted to make sure she would get more than two presents for Christmas. We all hopped in the Santa Mobile, as we had started calling the Jeep, and drove over to the young couple to whom we had given money for groceries. We looked quite the sight as we drove down the road: Santa and Mrs. Santa and two elves—with a car packed full of presents.

The elves helped me carry the bags up to the door, and after we knocked the young bride answered. We said, "This is so you'll have a fine Christmas dinner. Your husband told us you were a very good cook."

She looked at my Santa outfit and said, "You're the kind man who gave us the money in the grocery store. We made the comment at the grocery store that you looked like Santa. Now we know the truth!"

After hugs all around, we left her—still wearing a perplexed look on her face.

We next headed to the hospital only to find that little Amy had been released to go home. After telling the hospital about our mission they gladly gave us her home address, and we made the five-mile drive with Christmas carols playing and us singing.

When we arrived we went straight to the front door, still singing Christmas carols, and didn't even have to knock. Amy's mother had already opened the door to Santa and his three helpers laden with presents. We asked for Amy and were taken to a sofa in the front room where a beautiful little girl was watching the movie *Frozen* on the TV.

We greeted her with a "Merry Christmas!" and went to a Christmas tree that was as fine as I have ever seen, and deposited the gifts around it. We told Amy that she could open one of them tonight, but would have to wait until morning to discover what was in the others. She still wasn't too mobile, so in turn, we each gave her a kiss on the cheek.

Her reaction? "I told you Santa would come!"—along with a beautiful thank you.

Earlier, when we were at the hospital and found that Amy wasn't there, I alone went to Elizabeth's room. I walked in and could tell that she had taken the effort to pretty herself up for any potential Christmas visitors. As I walked in I said, "My, you look lovely!"

Elizabeth turned to see who might be visiting, and seemed to be very surprised that I was back.

I told her that I had brought her a reminder of the discussion we had during our last visit, and handed her a Christmas present wrapped with extra care in a petit box.

She said, "I love small presents. They're always the best." Then she asked if she could open it.

I nodded, and she very carefully removed the ribbon and paper as though they were made of gold. Inside she found a golden necklace with a pendant in the shape of a heart, a single gold wire that had three words inscribed into it. As you went around the heart it read, *Life Goes On.* It had so much meaning on so many levels that she appeared to read it over and over, and with each reading she became more emotional.

Finally she said, "I guess it's not time to think of giving up, is it?"

I merely said, "You have so much to offer." Then I wished her a very merry Christmas, and left.

We weren't too far from Kate's home, and we had made her gift a joint effort so we would deliver it together. Ann had said, "It has to be about memories." Mable added that it had to be "something that was very personal, and signified love." Sarah added that it had to be something lasting, that even when she grew old she could look on it with fond memories. I thought, *That is asking a lot of one small item.*

Ann, who seemed to always know where everything was to be found, had seen a beautiful piano music box in a Christmas store that played a different, delightfully arranged Christmas carol each time it was opened. It was made of porcelain and appeared as though it was made by a master craftsman. To make it play you merely lifted the piano lid. Its delicate nature and perfect form reminded us all of Kate.

We trooped up toward her front door, and before we had even gotten close she ran out to meet us.

Hers was a wonderful home. You could feel its spirit and warmth, and it wasn't long before we all had a cup of spiced apple cider and a Christmas cookie. We stated our intentions and presented our gift to Kate, along with heartfelt thanks for adding so much spirit to our own Christmas. It was an emotional time for us while we were all together.

Kate was so surprised when she opened her gift that it immediately brought on tears. She knew it was a gift over which had been given great thought. She stated simply: "I will cherish this and protect it the rest of my life. Every time it is played I will think of you."

She opened the lid and we listened to "It Came upon a Midnight Clear" to its finish, each of us lost in his or her own thoughts. Prolonged hugs and many tears brought the special occasion to an end.

I now had to get over to Mr. Clyde's. Kate handed each of us a package as we left, along with strict instructions not to open it until Christmas morning.

Fortunately, we had to pass our neighborhood on the way to Mr. Clyde's development. I dropped the girls off, reminding them that we still had business to finish when I got through with the Token of Appreciation presentation.

At the Edgemont Home Development I had been directed to meet them at the model home. There were two or three cars parked in the front, and I went in and was greeted by Mr. Clyde. He then introduced me to Danette who was his real estate company executive, and Mark Anderson who represented his legal department.

Mr. Clyde said, "Santa, I am making you a part of our exclusive club. Only you and we know what is about to happen. If you remain Santa over the years, we would like to have you take part in this endeavor. This won't happen every year but will come around almost bi-yearly. It is very important to me that we here are the only ones who know what is taking place. All sorts of chaos could result if this was made common knowledge. So, can you keep a secret?"

I said, "From everybody but my wife, and she loves and keeps secrets better than anyone I know."

He laughed a little and said, "I like your honesty, and believe that nothing should ever be kept secret between a husband and wife, so we're in agreement."

He then went on to tell me that with every home project he develops, he gives one home away to a worthy family. The home he gives is always the model home, furnished as it is to present a wonderful living environment. Danette always handles the real estate side of the transfer of ownership, and Mark makes it all legal. He told me that without violating a person's privacy, they gather data on those who visit the model home, and a family that could not otherwise even hope to afford such a home is presented with a clear title to the home of their dreams.

Mr. Clyde said, "We were wondering if you would present them with the keys and title to their new home."

I was astounded but very proud to be asked to participate in this great undertaking. I was then told that the family should be arriving at any moment.

It wasn't long before a mother and father pulled into the driveway. They had been told to leave their two young sons and a daughter at home. They had been drawn here on the guise of having won a drawing for a television set, which was offered to all visitors. Mr. Clyde and his associates had become very proficient at giving away homes and so it was fun to watch.

Mr. Clyde—or Wilford as I had been directed to call him, a very homespun type of a person with no airs about him—made the family feel very much at home, and guided them personally around the house once again. They ooh'd and ahh'd at every detail, and were once again dreaming of the day....

They arrived back at the living room and were seated and

were then presented with the TV. Wilford asked if they had a good spot to put it in, and was told they would find one.

Wilford then said, "We have a perfect spot for it!" and pointed to a corner in the family room.

The father said, "If only we could afford it."

Wilford then said, "Please steady yourself and take your wife firmly by the hand—she might need a little stabilizing. We would like to give you this home as you see it now, free and clear of all debt. You have been chosen not because of your needs, but because of your worthiness. Can you accept this as our gift to you?"

You've heard the statement, *It had to sink in.* This astonishing offer had to not only sink in but also had to be absorbed, gripped, soaked up, and understood in all its implications.

Mr. Clyde interrupted their astonished gaze by stating that there was one catch: "No one can ever know that you were given this home. You can tell them that special arrangements were made so you could afford it, but never that it was an outright gift. In other words, this is not to be publicized in any way. You will just seem to be another neighbor buying a home and moving in. There are no forfeitures if you do tell, but we want to keep doing this for a long time to come, and you can imagine the problems it would cause if this information got out. If agreeable, you can go pick up your kids and move in tonight if you want. It is all decorated for you to have a memorable Christmas."

Wow. We left this overwhelmed couple in Danette and Mark's able hands to finish up loose ends, and Wilford and I headed for Wilford's home. He had driven to the model home with Mark and so he accepted a ride with me to his home.

The time we spent conversing during the drive convinced me that in most ways Wilford was a very ordinary man. He had just determined that there was more to life than building homes, that the more he built the better he got, and that the better he got the more he had to offer.

I then shared with him my personal quest for being the real Santa, and told him that his example of being a real person went a long way in convincing me that I still had hope.

By the time we drove into his driveway the TV truck and crew and the newspaper staff were already gathered. He looked at me and said, "This is going to be a little bigger than I thought it was, isn't it?"

I told him that he would be getting some free commercial time out of this, and we both laughed. But then he looked a little questionably at me, and knowing what he was thinking, I assured him that his secret was still safe with me.

I grabbed my bag and we went right into his living room. I noticed that his home was large but not ostentatious. His family had gathered and we had a wonderful time as he introduced me to all of them. I had many bags of candy and made sure they all got one. The TV and newspaper crews were invited in and became part of the family.

When I was given the floor, I announced that each year one citizen out of our community was chosen by Santa Claus and presented with an award. This award was a token of appreciation for the chosen one's significant contribution to the community. This year, their husband, father, and grandfather had been chosen to receive this award. I then proceeded to read the engraved plaque that the coin was attached to:

*This Token of Appreciation is presented to*

## Mr. Wilford Clyde

*Who through his care and consideration, has provided many quality homes for our community.*

*His attention to detail and revisits to each homeowner to make certain everything is acceptable has endeared and deeply indebted us to him.*

*This token also recognizes his many anonymous gifts— given not out of obligation, but out of kindness.*

*Thank you, Mr. Clyde. We are a better community because of you.*

We handed him the coin and the plaque it fit in. He was moved and maybe a little embarrassed as the cameramen took the pictures they needed to tell their stories. After saying my goodbyes with a promise to stay in touch, I was off to my next duty.

I had to go back to the hospital. I'd wished that I could have taken care of it on my previous visit, but the paperwork I needed had not arrived. I had contacted a company called Pure Movement Prosthetics. I explained to them Jesse's problem and asked if they would give me a cost—after insurance, of what an arm for Jesse would cost. I assured them that I would be taking care of the bill, and asked if it were at all possible to have a gift of the arm given, in writing, from their company. They told me they would have the paperwork dropped off at the information desk of the hospital and I could pick it up there.

This time, the letter had arrived and said what I needed it to say:

*This is to guarantee Jesse Ewell one left micro-electric arm controlled by muscle movements, with a functioning artificial hand, to be delivered upon request at no cost to him or his parents.*

*Pure Movement Prosthetics*
*Mr. Duane Hudson, President*

I went to Jesse's room, knowing well that on Christmas Eve his parents would be with him. I entered a room to find the mother reading out of a book to Jesse and his father.

Jesse saw me first and perked right up. He said "Santa!" and I soon had everyone's attention.

I said, "Before I started on my rounds tonight, I wanted to stop by and bring you a very special present." I handed Jesse the envelope, and he pulled out the letter.

He couldn't read it yet so handed it to his mother. She glanced over the letter, and tears came to her eyes before she started reading aloud. She said, "Listen to this!" and read the letter.

It was no surprise to me to see both the mother and father crying, while Jesse had a big smile on his face.

I soon left and drove back home to pick up my wife and my elves. We had three more stops to make before we finished this year's Christmas season.

I had asked Ann earlier if she had come up with any ideas of how to help Mindy Crandall have a happy family. Ann said, "From her letter, we were never told why they were unhappy. It's hard to figure out what to do to make them happy when you don't know why they're not. Well, Mable and I did a reconnaissance. We actually parked across the street from their home and tried to get an idea of what was going on. They live in a nice neighborhood and seem to live a very normal life.

"One day while we were watching, Mrs. Crandall pulled into her driveway and started carrying groceries into the house. I ran across the street and introduced myself to her and told her we worked with Santa Claus. I pulled out Mindy's letter and let her read it."

"Mrs. Crandall said, 'We read her letter before we let her send it. We weren't too concerned about it because she is a very happy child. We never thought anyone ever read the letters.' Then she very apologetically said, 'Oh! What must you think of us! Mindy's problem is that she is an only child, and as you can see, we are taking care of that.'"

"At that she turned sideways, and we understood. Mrs. Crandall told us she has very difficult pregnancies and always has very bad morning sickness. And yes, it did make her husband worry a lot."

Ann said, "We sent Mindy a letter in return and told her that soon Santa would be sending her a special gift, and their whole family would be very happy. Our visit ended on a high note."

Previously, I had approached a television production studio and told them of my problem with the little girl who had lost her father two months ago. They assured me there were many things they could do to keep her father's memory alive. If they could collect any family movies that had been made, and even still pictures of her father, they could put a collage together on a DVD of his life, one that could be played anytime the family wanted to remember him.

Collecting this material before Christmas would defeat the purpose of surprise, and so it was decided that a certificate would be given to the girl and her mother for this work to be completed right after Christmas. We had picked up the certificate and had also purchased several presents for both of them.

The little girl and her mother were more than surprised when they saw us at their front door. We were invited in, and we made certain they were given the attention needed. After distributing the packages, I handed the mother the envelope containing the certificate and explained our intentions.

She said, "I so want to have his memory preserved for my daughter. I have movies and pictures that can be used."

I assured her the studio was very professional, and all the costs had been taken care of. I said, "Your husband might be lost, but he will never be forgotten.

As we were leaving the little girl said, "See, Mom, there is a solution."

On to our next delivery. Earlier, I had gone to the camera store where we bought Eddie's camera and found out that with a certain plug-in device that they had, the camera could be plugged into any modern TV and the pictures could be shown on the big screen. Thinking that this might enhance Eddie's and Jamie's relationship greatly, I purchased the device, but I couldn't remember seeing a television in Jamie's room. So I went to a store in the mall and purchased a 32-inch smart television.

When we arrived at Jamie's house, Eddie's wasn't there but had left the camera with Jamie. We all went in, and I introduced my wife and my elves. We set up the television and I demonstrated the camera as I had been shown.

A whole new world immediately opened up to Jamie and he just couldn't wait to show Eddie. He picked up the phone and called Eddie: "You've got to get right over here. You won't believe what I just got!"

We dismissed ourselves in spite of our preoccupation in watching pictures, and left for our next appointment.

It was getting late in the afternoon, and Mable told me we had to be at our next appointment at 5 p.m. For some reason they had kept from me whom we would be meeting. I noticed that they had brought a large box that seemed to have been wrapped with extra care.

On the way I was told that we were going to visit Mrs. B. Unbeknownst to me, Mable had found out through her sleuthing that several of Mrs. B's family would be at the assembly. She had approached them individually and asked if they would send photos of Mrs. B during different phases of her life, especially classroom and children's photos.

Mable had found a way of printing photos from the computer onto different-sized fabrics. She intended to make what she called a *memory quilt*. I found out later that Mable had made a patchwork quilt out of all these pictures, one that could be used to comfort Mrs. B while she read or watched TV.

I could see when we drove up that several others had been notified of our arrival. We knocked on the door and were taken directly to Mrs. B. We gave our season's greetings and were offered a cup of hot chocolate and some cookies. As I thought of it, we hadn't eaten for quite some time and so this tasted particularly good.

Mrs. B was the first to address us directly and said, "You must be the Santa that Mark has told me so much about. He was very adamant in letting me know that the real Santa had helped plan my reward, and I thank you. Wasn't it wonderful?"

I just wanted to pause and sit at this lady's feet and glean the wisdom of her years of service. There was much for a Santa to learn here. I told her that my elves had made her a special gift and that they now would like to present it to her.

After a discussion of "You do it,— no you do it!" where the box kept getting passed around, it was finally left to Mable to give her this gift. Mable handed Mrs. B the large gift and she opened it with care. The family gathered as closely as possible to see what it was.

Mrs. B opened it to reveal the beautiful patchwork quilt, hand stitched, with over 40 pictures displayed on both sides. There were pictures of her as a little girl, as a teenager, and as a young teacher in front of her first class. Pets, Christmas trees, cars, dolls, dresses, and cakes she had baked were all presented on this quilt.

We had finally given Mrs. B something that struck her dumb—she had absolutely nothing to say. At first, there was silence as she looked at each picture, and then tears followed as she wrapped herself in this gift of love. Mrs. Santa and the elves had earned their reward for all their hard work.

We now looked forward to our last stop of the day. Believe me when I tell you that by this time we were all exhausted. We called this final visit our "manger visit." Ann kept looking up to the sky to see if there just might be a special star twinkling.

We stopped by Mary and Jacob's home, and with arms loaded with wrapped presents of all sizes, we knocked on the door and were graciously invited in.

Mary had decided that their new son should be shown in all his glory. She had placed a cradle in the corner of the living room and had surrounded it with stuffed animals the babe had already received, and there he lay in his cradle. I wouldn't have been at all surprised if a light from a star really had shone through the window to light up the scene.

Not many words were spoken as we gathered around the cradle. I reflected, *This is a sacred experience. How I feel now cannot be much different than how the shepherds felt around the baby Jesus.*

We then offered our gifts to Mary. Unlike today, I don't recall that there were thanks given when the first gifts were presented. There wasn't a need for it as it would have just interfered with that solemn occasion. Among the gifts today was a small wallet-sized box that contained two bills marked *"Paid In Full."*

Their child was beautiful and we drank in the wonderful newness of the baby. Controlling our desires to hold him, we let him sleep on. Staying only a few minutes, we left the family alone. That sounded nice to us, to have this family spend their first Christmas Eve together.

# 51

## *Being Santa*

I was about to drop Ann and Mable off on my way home, but it seemed like it would be a little anti-climactic. I knew they were worn to a frazzle, but I just couldn't see them going home to an empty house alone. The truth of the matter was that I loved these two dear ladies, and a moment together with them seemed appropriate. When I told them that I knew they were tired but asked if they would mind spending just a little time together to enjoy the end of a great Christmas season, they seemed to perk up and thought it was a good idea.

Mable said, "I wouldn't sleep anyway. I would just lie there and think of all the wonderful things that have happened."

Back at out home, we sat around our kitchen table and had a slice of pie and a glass of milk and just enjoyed each other's company. But eventually, all good things must come to an end. I walked them both home and another Christmas season had come to an end.

Back home Sarah and I fussed around a little. Both of us managed to sneak our presents under the tree for Christmas morning, and we soon found our way to bed. It felt good to finally lie down. We had the best bed in the world, and it always felt so good to snuggle under the covers and just drift off to sleep. Sarah hit the pillow and was gone.

The problem for me was that I wasn't drifting. I was thinking. It wasn't visions of sugarplums that were keeping me awake; it was visions of being Santa. *Had I done it? Had I been Santa?*

I would like to have been able to dream that I was Santa Claus, delivering gifts around the world. And when I awoke I'd like to wonder: *Am I a man who just dreamt of being Santa Claus, or am I Santa Claus, who just dreamt of being a man?* I would prefer there to be very little distinction between those two dreams.

The best thing about being Santa is that you are loved—even before others meet you. Probably the worst thing about being Santa is not deserving that love. I couldn't imagine being a Santa in whom someone was disappointed.

I acknowledged again that I had to be real to myself before I could ever be real to anyone else. I had also come to understand the principle that real living includes living for others.

I then asked myself, *Am I a better person for having become Santa?*

The answer was yes. I was better. But I was still far from perfect. Oh, I may have experienced moments of seeming perfection, but I had also learned that *attaining* perfection *and retaining it* seemed impossible for now.

I reflected on those moments of seeming perfection such as the song sung by Kate—flawless in its presentation, but when repeated later might not quite be the same. I embraced the idea that experiencing even one brief moment of perfection was worth every effort.

As I began to finally drift off I thought, *I believe I have been Santa to the best of my ability.*

There certainly is much more to learn. And I have time.

*The End*